Fear & Folklore:
American Monsters

Allen Sircy

Table of Contents

Introduction 3

Bigfoot 5

Beasts of the Northeast 14

Creatures of the Southeast 39

Midwest Monsters 97

Southwest Legends 116

Cryptids of the West 137

Northwest Lore 152

Hoaxes 173

Introduction

When I was a kid, I used to go spend the night with my grandmother at least once a week. While I was at her house, she always had several of the top tabloids from the supermarket like the National Enquirer and Star. However, the love lives of Burt Reynolds and Dolly Parton failed to pique my interest. Instead, I found myself irresistibly drawn to the Weekly World News, with its outrageously exaggerated headlines that demanded attention.

Aliens abducting a sasquatch? Oh man!

A real-life bat-boy hybrid? Yes, please!

A giant squid attacking the coast of New Jersey? That's awesome!

Bigfoot steals a racecar. Take my money!

Since 2018, I've been writing ghost stories, a passion that has taken me on a journey into the world of the supernatural. However, as the years rolled by, my curiosity led me to explore monsters and cryptids, inspired by stories that I stumbled upon in old newspapers. These stories introduced me to creatures like "The Mississippi River Monster" in New Orleans and "The Atlantic City Sea Serpent." While ghost stories are undeniably enjoyable, there's something truly captivating about a tale featuring a living, breathing monster.

I understand that stories passed down through generations may have been embellished and expanded upon to sound more grandiose. But monsters and cryptids are as American as apple pie. Stories of the Jersey Devil and Bigfoot have endured for years, and discerning fact from fiction can be quite the challenge. These creatures are born from stories and legends passed down through decades, and sometimes even centuries. While not every detail may be 100% factual, each creature in this book has left a documented trail over the years.

Some, like the Mothman, have amassed a devoted following, while others, such as the Hendersonville Shadow and The Stench, have only been whispered about in hushed, smaller circles.

So, here it is - "American Monsters and Legends." I hope you enjoy reading it as much as I did writing it!

Bigfoot

In the realm of cryptids and mysterious creatures, one towering figure reigns supreme—the elusive Bigfoot. The history of Bigfoot, the mysterious ape-like creature said to inhabit the wilderness of North America, is a tale that spans decades and has captivated the public's imagination. The fascination with Bigfoot has led to numerous investigations, sightings, and a deep-rooted cultural impact that has endured through the years.

Bigfoot is not a modern phenomenon; indigenous cultures in North America have stories and legends about large, human-like creatures dating back centuries. Among these is the legend of the "Sasquatch" in the Pacific Northwest, particularly among tribes like the Salish, Lummi, and Kwakwaka'wakw. These early accounts describe large, hairy, and often elusive beings inhabiting the remote forests.

It was 1811 in the wilderness of what's now known as the state of Washington. Explorer David Thompson, renowned for mapping the uncharted North American frontier, had an encounter that would etch his name into cryptozoology history.

As Thompson ventured deep into the wild, he and his expedition party stumbled upon peculiar tracks in the mud, tracks unlike any animal they'd ever seen. These footprints were large, human-like, yet far larger and more imposing.

Thompson recorded the event meticulously in his journal, describing the prints as measuring a whopping 14 inches in length! He pondered the possibility of a gigantic, undiscovered primate roaming the American wilderness—a creature later dubbed "Sasquatch" by the indigenous people.

The legend of Bigfoot was born, and Thompson's account ignited curiosity and speculation.

The term "Bigfoot" was popularized in the 1950s, notably after a series of encounters in Bluff Creek, California. It gained widespread attention when a construction worker named Jerry Crew discovered unusual footprints at a logging site in 1958. Crew cast these tracks in plaster and shared them with the media, coining the term "Bigfoot" for the creature. These plaster casts created a sensation and were crucial in launching Bigfoot into public consciousness.

One of the most famous and controversial moments in Bigfoot history is the Patterson-Gimlin film of 1967.

The Patterson-Gimlin film, also known as the PG film, was shot by Roger Patterson and Robert Gimlin in the Bluff Creek region of Northern California. The two men were amateur Bigfoot researchers who believed that this remote area was home to the elusive creature. They embarked on their expedition with hopes of providing definitive proof of Bigfoot's existence.

On the afternoon of October 20, 1967, Patterson and Gimlin were riding horses in the untamed wilderness of Bluff Creek. The forest seemed to hold endless secrets, and they were determined to uncover them. Suddenly, as they turned a bend, they came upon an astonishing sight: a large, hair-covered figure walking away from them along the creek's sandbar.

Patterson, who was on horseback, quickly dismounted and grabbed his 16mm camera. His shaky hands struggled to load a roll of film. This marked the beginning of a 59.5-second film that would change the course of Bigfoot research. Gimlin, on horseback, remained still, providing stability for the camera.

The resulting footage showed a female Sasquatch striding along the creek, glancing back over her shoulder at the two astonished men. Patterson and Gimlin maintained that they followed the creature for about a minute until she disappeared into the woods.

Following the sighting, Patterson and Gimlin reached out to experts and scientists to analyze the film. Grover Krantz, a respected anthropologist, was one of the first to conduct a detailed study of the footage. Despite doubts and skepticism, Krantz concluded that the film was genuine, and monster's features were biologically consistent with a female Sasquatch.

The PG film immediately faced skepticism and criticism. Some claimed it was an elaborate hoax, suggesting that the Bigfoot was simply a man in a costume. Critics pointed to issues like the clear view of the beast's breasts and the lack of any anatomical inconsistencies.

The Patterson-Gimlin film has since become the most famous and controversial piece of evidence in Bigfoot research. It has been analyzed, dissected, and debated for decades. While some believe it's a legitimate glimpse of a Sasquatch, others maintain it's a well-executed hoax.

The legacy of the PG film continues to influence Bigfoot investigations and enthusiasts, inspiring documentaries, books, and TV shows. The debate over its authenticity remains a central point of contention within the Bigfoot research community.

While many claim that the PG film is legitimate, the scientific community remains highly skeptical of Bigfoot's existence. Several high-profile hoaxes, including the infamous "Bigfoot in a Freezer" incident, have added fuel to the skepticism. The year 2008 witnessed one of the most audacious and bizarre episodes in the annals of cryptozoology. A tale of astounding proportions shook the world: a purported "Bigfoot corpse" discovered in a freezer.

It all began in August 2008 when two men, Matthew Whitton and Rick Dyer, held a press conference in Palo Alto, California, announcing a shocking discovery.

Whitton and Dyer appeared in front of an audience with a large, refrigerated container that supposedly housed the elusive creature's frozen remains. The dramatic unveiling captured the world's attention, with news outlets and enthusiasts descending upon the scene. The promise of scientific validation for the existence of Bigfoot hung palpably in the air.

With the spotlight firmly on them, Whitton and Dyer began their story. They claimed to have found the lifeless creature in the Georgia wilderness, and the monster's body, they asserted, had been preserved in a block of ice. However, the evidence presented raised eyebrows among skeptics who noticed several red flags, including the suspiciously low-quality photos of the "corpse."

As the days passed, it became increasingly apparent that the entire spectacle was a hoax. Skeptics and experts alike pointed out numerous inconsistencies in the story and photographic evidence. In a shocking twist, it was revealed that Whitton and Dyer had a history of fraud and run-ins with the law.

As journalists and cryptozoologists delved deeper into the case, their story fell apart. Whitton and Dyer's credibility took a nosedive, and their tall tale became the laughingstock of mainstream media.

The climax of the Bigfoot in a Freezer saga occurred when the freezer was finally opened, and the supposed creature's remains were revealed. To the dismay of hopeful enthusiasts and the satisfaction of skeptics, the truth was laid bare. Inside the freezer lay not a cryptid Bigfoot, but a life-sized gorilla suit, propped against a backdrop of crushed ice.

The entire ruse had been a hoax, from start to finish. Whitton and Dyer had managed to dupe both the media and the public for a brief but attention-grabbing moment in the history of Bigfoot folklore.

Following their exposure, Whitton and Dyer faced public ridicule and legal repercussions. The story of the Bigfoot in a Freezer not only highlighted the potential for deceit in cryptozoological pursuits but also made skeptics more vigilant about claims of extraordinary discoveries.

Interest in Bigfoot persists, and there is a dedicated community of researchers and enthusiasts who continue their quest to prove the creature's existence. Some scientists engage in rigorous, albeit unconventional, investigations to gather evidence and test hypotheses.

As technology advances and the search for answers continues, the legend of Bigfoot is sure to evolve, keeping this elusive cryptid a prominent figure in the realm of the unknown.

Bigfoot has left an indelible mark on popular culture, inspiring numerous books, documentaries, and television shows, such as "Finding Bigfoot" and "MonsterQuest." It has also influenced films like "Harry and the Hendersons" and has become the most beloved character in the cryptid world.

Beasts of the Northeast

Champy

Champy, the legendary lake monster of Lake Champlain, has captivated the imaginations of people for centuries, weaving a rich tapestry of sightings and folklore. This mysterious creature, often described as a massive, Loch Ness monster-like being, gracefully gliding through the dark waters of Lake Champlain, has left an indelible mark on the history and culture of the region.

Lake Champlain, is a massive freshwater lake straddling the border between Vermont and New York. It dwarfs renowned locations like Loch Ness and Okanagan Lake, stretching over 125 miles in length, with an additional 6 miles extending into Quebec, Canada. The lake is bordered by New York to the west and Vermont to the east.

The Indigenous people who have long inhabited the Lake Champlain region, including the Abenaki and the Iroquois, have their own stories of a large lake-dwelling creature. In Abenaki tradition, this creature is known as Gitaskog, resembling a horned serpent or giant snake. During the early 18th century, Abenakis cautioned French explorers not to disturb the waters of the lake, to avoid agitating the serpent.

Samuel de Champlain, after whom the lake is named, is sometimes mistakenly credited with being the first European to spot Champy. However, his accounts actually describe a sighting near the St. Lawrence River. The term "Champy" or "Champ" actually originated from an entry in his diary in 1609, where he described seeing the sea serpent in Lake Champlain.

His description of the creature was noteworthy. He described it as follows: "there is also a great abundance of many species of fish. Amongst others there is one called by the natives Chaousarou, which is of various lengths; but the largest of them, as these tribes have told me, are from eight to ten feet long." He noted its head was as large as his two fists, with a snout of 2.5 feet and a double row of sharp teeth. Its body resembled a pike, covered in strong, silvery-gray scales.

Reports of Champy sightings have continued over the years, providing detailed descriptions. In 1819, Captain P. Crum claimed to see a black monster approximately 187 feet long with distinct features in the lake. In 1873, there were multiple sightings, including one by a railroad crew and another by the passengers of the steamship W.B. Eddy, which had a close encounter with Champy. Even showman P. T. Barnum offered a substantial reward for the hide of the great Champlain serpent.

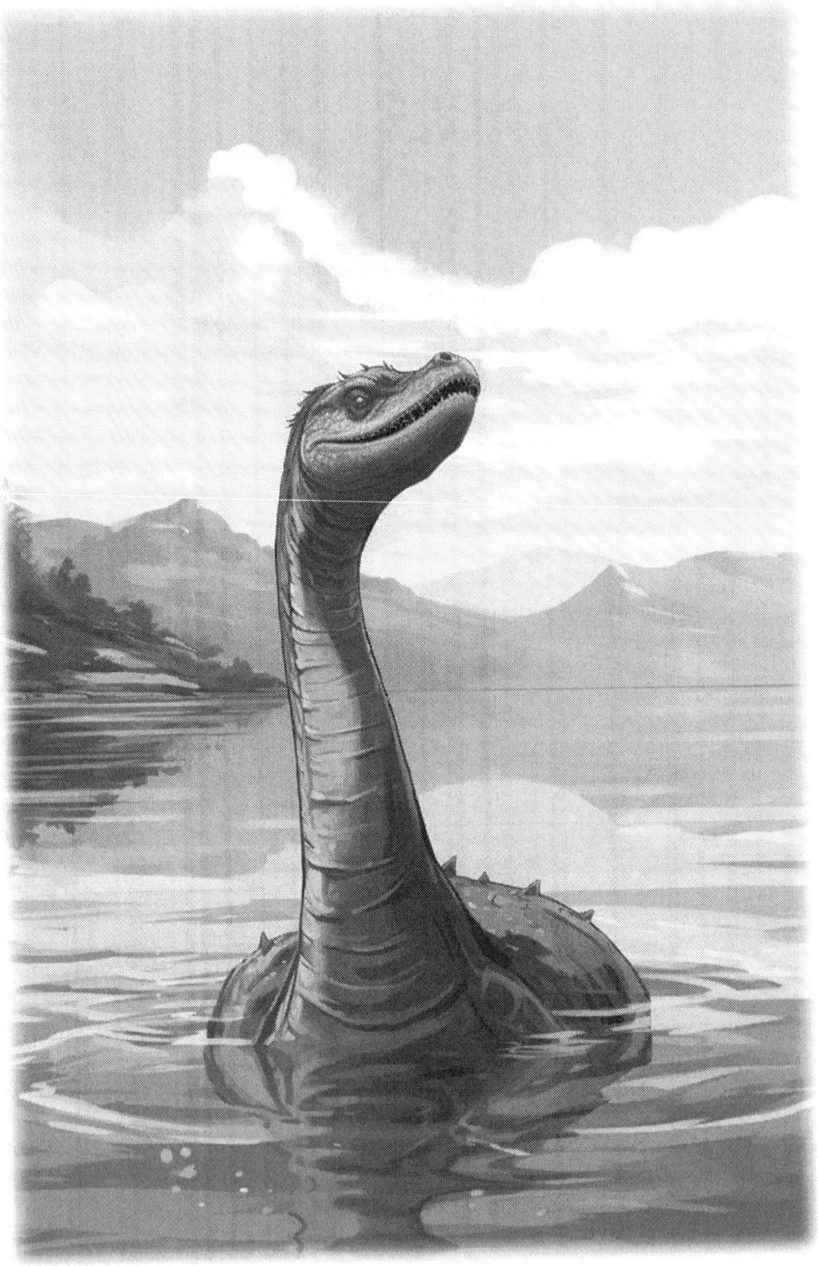

By 1992, there were approximately 180 sightings, with about 600 people claiming to have encountered Champy. The 21st century brought a resurgence of sightings, attracting attention from various media outlets.

Champy has become not only a creature of folklore but also a symbol of regional identity and pride. The legal protection of Champy highlights the cultural significance and reverence with which the creature is regarded.

In 1981, Port Henry, New York, took the initiative to declare their waters a safe haven for Champy. This local resolution was an early step in recognizing the significance of Champy to the community. The state of Vermont passed a House Resolution in 1982, marking a formal acknowledgment of Champy's importance within the state's culture and heritage. This resolution served to ensure that Champy would be protected on the Vermont side of Lake Champlain. In 1983, both the New York State Assembly and the New York State Senate passed resolutions, collectively declaring the need to protect the creature. These legislative actions underscored the bipartisan recognition of Champy as a cultural icon transcending state boundaries.

Today, Champ is celebrated throughout the region, whether real or mythical. In Vermont, there's a baseball team called the Lake Monsters with a Champy mascot. A Champy statue graces Port Henry, New York, and images of the friendly monster can be found on various merchandise, children's books, and historic markers, commemorating the enduring legacy of everyone's favorite lake monster.

The Coos County Woods Devils

In the remote and densely wooded landscapes of Coos County, New Hampshire, a mysterious and eerie presence has haunted the locals for decades – the mysterious Woods Devils. Since the 1930s, stories of these elusive creatures, described as tall and skinny, akin to the legendary Bigfoot, have been spotted in the hills and forests of the region.

The Woods Devils, whether singular or part of a group, are often said to stand between 7 to 9 feet in height, towering over the average human. They possess a slender and nimble frame, their bodies enveloped in a shaggy coat of gray fur. Their presence in the wilderness is marked by their ability to remain hidden, blending seamlessly with the natural surroundings.

These beings are renowned for their elusiveness, with sightings often occurring when least expected. They are masters of stealth and adaptability, capable of swiftly moving from one tree to another, utilizing their agility to evade detection. Their most peculiar trait is their uncanny ability to stand still, frozen like a statue against the trunk of a tree when confronted by a human presence. This strategy allows them to hide in plain sight, almost imperceptible to the untrained eye. Even when cover is not available, these creatures remain immobile, waiting until they are confident that they have been spotted.

These monsters exhibit carnivorous tendencies, preying on small animals like rabbits and rodents. During the harsh winter months when food is scarce, they turn to scavenging, often feeding on carrion – the carcasses of dead animals. In their quest for food, they may occasionally raid garbage cans or target livestock.

Adding to their air of mystery, the Woods Devils are known for their loud screams and howls that pierce through the hollows and valleys of Coos County. These eerie sounds, echoing in the night, are thought to serve as a form of communication or a territorial display, intensifying the mystique surrounding these creatures.

For decades, the legends of the Woods Devils have persisted in the remote corners of Coos County, captivating the imagination of those who call this region home.

The Dover Demon

In the quiet and quaint town of Dover, Massachusetts, a mysterious and unsettling figure emerged from the shadows to cast a spell of uncertainty over the community. This mysterious beast, known as the "Dover Demon," has left an indelible mark on local lore and continues to intrigue and perplex those who live in Delaware.

The story begins in the spring of 1977 when a series of strange and bewildering sightings rattled the otherwise peaceful town. It was during this time that three separate individuals claimed to have encountered a creature that defied explanation and eluded classification.

Descriptions of the Dover Demon varied slightly among the witnesses, but certain traits remained consistent. The creature was said to be small in stature, standing no taller than three feet, with matted fur that appeared to be reflective in the moonlight. Its most distinctive feature, however, were its large, round head and disproportionately large, glowing orange eyes that seemed to penetrate the darkness with an eerie and hypnotic intensity.

The first sighting occurred when a 17-year-old boy was driving along Farm Street late at night. He claimed to have seen a small, unearthly figure hunched by the side of the road. Startled and curious, he observed the creature for several moments before it reportedly scampered away, disappearing into the night. He later recounted his experience to friends, who were skeptical yet intrigued by his story.

The second sighting took place the following evening when another teenager, this time a 15-year-old girl, reported seeing a similar creature while walking with friends near Miller Hill Road. Her description of the Dover Demon's glowing eyes and unusual appearance matched the previous account.

The third and final sighting occurred just hours after the second. A young man driving along Springdale Avenue spotted a small, eerie figure sitting on a stone wall. Struck by the creature's unsettling presence, he later described its strange appearance to local authorities.

In the days that followed, the Dover Demon became the subject of intense speculation and discussion within the town and beyond. Skeptics suggested that the sightings could be attributed to misidentifications of an animal or simple pranks, while believers clung to the notion that an otherworldly entity had indeed made its presence known.

The Dover Demon, despite its fleeting appearances and lack of physical evidence, became a source of fascination for cryptozoologists, paranormal enthusiasts, and curious locals alike.

As the years passed, the legend only grew in intensity, and the creature's legacy remained a defining aspect of Dover Demon's identity.

The Glocester Ghoul

In the late summer of 1839, Albert Hicks and his gang of scoundrels, fueled by tales of Captain Kidd's treasure, embarked on a daring expedition to Paige Farm in Glocester, Rhode Island. Armed with shovels and picks, they began digging in the hopes of uncovering the fabled stash. However, their endeavors were abruptly halted by a spine-tingling sound emanating from the darkness of the surrounding forest. Paralyzed by fear, they dropped their tools and gazed in terror at the unearthly horror that emerged from the shadows.

Hicks, trembling as he recounted the nightmarish encounter, described the creature as an abomination. Its eyes glowed with an eerie intensity, akin to balls of fire, and as it exhaled, flames spewed from its mouth and nostrils, leaving a scorched trail through the underbrush. This creature, unlike anything they had ever imagined, dwarfed a cow in size, boasting dark wings reminiscent of a bats and spiral horns akin to a ram's, each as wide as a stovepipe.

Its feet were webbed like a duck's, spanning a foot and a half, and its body was encased in scales as large as clamshells, creating a disconcerting rattling noise as it moved. Mysterious lights pierced through its sides, casting an otherworldly glow like lanterns.

Even before they laid eyes on this grotesque entity, Hicks and his companions could sense its presence, an oppressive feeling accompanied by a strange burnt wool-like odor. It seemed to manifest out of thin air and then vanish as swiftly as it had appeared, leaving them awestruck and paralyzed by terror.

This eerie encounter left the treasure hunters in a state of perpetual dread, and they vowed never to return to Paige Farm, uncertain about whether they had encountered a hellhound guarding Kidd's loot riches or one of the eerie creatures that local lore spoke of, inhabiting the swamps and deep forests nearby.

Decades passed, and the story of the Glocester Ghoul faded into local legend. But in 1896, the unnerving creature resurfaced, this time witnessed by a local named Neil Hopkins. His chilling encounter, recounted in the pages of The Evening Hour, sent ripples through the community.

Neil's harrowing experience occurred on a bitterly cold winter evening as he made his way home from Putnam, Connecticut. Despite being familiar with the route and having traveled it countless times, this night was different. He couldn't shake a sense of unease. As he approached the darkest stretch of his journey, a peculiar sound echoed from the depths of the forest, drawing closer with each passing moment. Suddenly, as if emerging from a portal to the netherworld, a supernatural beast charged forth from the shadows, relentlessly pursuing him.

The creature appeared to be engulfed in flames and emitted searing heat, and a metallic clanking sound reverberated through the air as it moved. Neil, his heart pounding with terror, described the beast as colossal, nearly the size of an elephant, yet curiously lacking a tail.

The beast gave chase but eventually veered off into the woods, leaving Neil to listen to the creepy symphony of cracking branches and twigs.

The town was left baffled by the mysterious apparition, with some speculating that it might have been a bear, while others wondered if it was the infamous "burning beast" that had haunted Glocester since Albert Hicks's fateful encounter 57 years earlier.

Since then, the legend of the Glocester Ghoul has endured, casting a perpetual shadow of fear over this cursed corner of Rhode Island.

The Mysterious Sea Serpent of Atlantic City

In the late summer of 1894, a group of men stationed at the Atlantic City Life Saving Station were going about their routine duties along the serene shores. Little did they know that their peaceful day would take an astonishing turn. As they gazed out across the sparkling expanse of the ocean, their attention was suddenly captured by an incredible sight. A massive black sea serpent, an enigmatic creature from the depths of maritime legends, was gracefully navigating the coastal waters. Its long, sinuous body cut through the waves, giving rise to both awe and trepidation among the crew.

The men's initial wonderment quickly turned to fear as the sheer size of the creature became apparent. Fearing for their safety, the startled crew members grabbed hold of their pistols and, with trembling hands, began firing shots into the water. The cracking sounds echoed across the beach, and some of the bullets struck the creature, causing it to writhe and thrash in the water. Despite the harrowing spectacle, the crew's concerted efforts seemed to have an effect; the sea serpent altered its course and started to swim away from the shore and out to sea.

In the aftermath of the encounter, the story of the crew's confrontation with the sea serpent spread throughout the community. The brave actions of the Life Saving Station's men were hailed as heroic, their pistols and courage having successfully turned away the mysterious beast.

Fast forward to August 14, 1896, Captain Charles Peterson, a seasoned seaman who had traversed the oceans for decades, was aboard a steamboat in the Atlantic, not far from the shores of Atlantic City. The captain and his crew were engaged in a filibustering expedition, their focus and anticipation aimed at the uncharted horizons that stretched before them.

Amidst the expanse of the open ocean, a sense of adventure mingled with the salty breeze. Yet, the tranquility of the moment was shattered by a sudden burst of excitement from one of Peterson's crew members. Urgently, the crewman pointed to a sight that defied belief—a quarter mile away, a colossal jet-black sea serpent was gracefully gliding through the waves. Its head, resembling that of a horse, was held high as it moved with an air of graceful majesty. The creature's sheer magnitude inspired both awe and disbelief among those who bore witness.

The sea serpent remained visible for an astonishing 30 minutes, its presence capturing the attention of Captain Peterson and his crew. The seasoned seaman was no stranger to the mysteries of the ocean, yet the enormity of the creature before him left him speechless. Eventually, the sea serpent's form dipped beneath the waves, disappearing momentarily from view. As if carried by a tide of curiosity and courage, Peterson followed its movements with a mixture of fear and fascination.

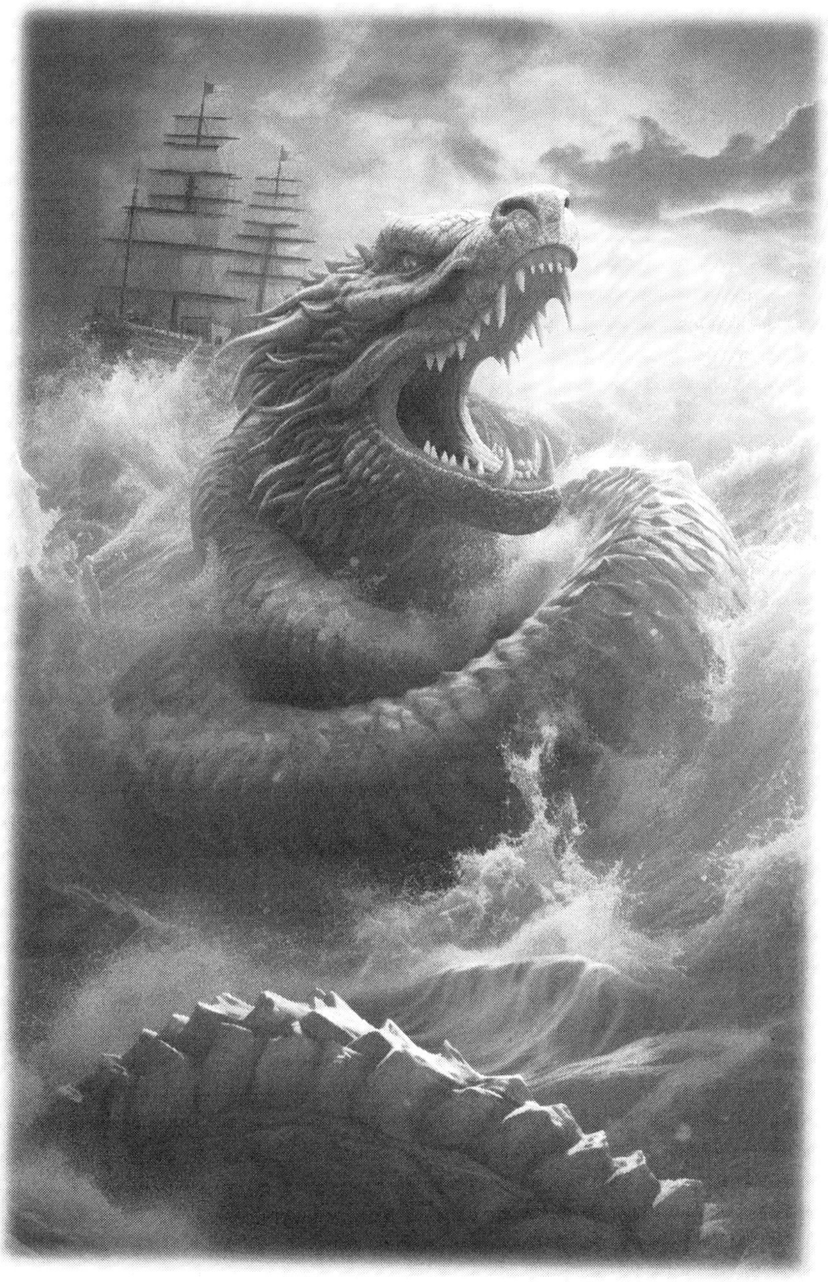

The creature, seemingly aware of the attention it had garnered, maintained its submerged course, its head concealed beneath the waves. The once-vibrant, horse-like head of the sea serpent remained hidden, allowing only tantalizing glimpses of its immense form to breach the surface. Peterson's heart raced as he tracked the creature's path.

Time passed, and the sea serpent continued its journey. Eventually, its path shifted, and it gradually turned away from the coast, setting a course toward the open sea. Peterson watched as the creature's jet-black form retreated into the distance, gradually becoming a silhouette against the endless expanse of water and sky.

News of Captain Peterson's extraordinary encounter soon rippled through Atlantic City. Initially met with skepticism, the story gained traction when two members of Peterson's own crew came forward to corroborate the captain's account. Their testimony lent credence to the fantastical tale.

For a time, the tale of the colossal sea serpent reverberated throughout Atlantic City, captivating the minds of both residents and visitors. As the narrative spread, so did a sense of unease. The waters that had once been a source of leisure and refreshment suddenly held a newfound air of mystery and apprehension. For weeks, people hesitated to dip even a toe into the ocean, cautious of the shadow that the sea serpent's presence had cast over their beloved shores.

Yet, as weeks turned into months, and the sea serpent's appearances remained elusive, a cautious sense of normalcy returned. Slowly, the beaches saw the return of laughter, the waters welcomed the splashes of carefree swimmers, and life by the shore continued its steady rhythm.

The sea serpent had retreated back into the depths from whence it came, leaving behind a trail of awe, fear, and wonder.

The Jersey Devil

Tucked away in the New Jersey Pine Barrens, an eerie and captivating legend was born many years ago — the legendary Jersey Devil. Its origin, deeply intertwined with folklore, finds its roots in the 18th century and begins with a woman named Mother Leeds, living in the Pine Barrens. Expecting her thirteenth child, she uttered a fateful declaration in frustration, wishing the child to be the devil. From that moment, the Jersey Devil was said to have been conceived.

According to the myth, the creature was born as an ordinary infant but quickly metamorphosed into a grotesque and terrifying entity. Possessing hooves, wings, a horse-like head, and a forked tail, it spread fear and chaos as it roamed the land.

Over the years, sightings have poured in from all over New Jersey. Descriptions painted the creature as having a kangaroo-like body, bat-like wings, a horse-like head, sharp claws, and eerie glowing red eyes. It was said to emit a spine-chilling screech that struck fear into those who heard it.

The most notorious wave of Jersey Devil sightings occurred in 1909, spreading fear across New Jersey and eastern Pennsylvania. Schools closed, factories shut down, and people searched anxiously for the elusive creature in the woods and swamps. One fisherman off the coast of Atlantic City even falsely claimed to have captured the Jersey Devil after catching a large bird in a fishing net. However, during this chaotic time, no concrete evidence was ever found of the fabled monster, and the frenzy gradually subsided.

Ten years later, Frank Adams, the keeper of the Absecon Lighthouse, claimed to have encountered the Jersey Devil. He spotted the creature perched atop the lighthouse, prompting him to take action. Adams fired his weapon, striking the creature. The aftermath was surreal, with haunting wails filling the air as the wounded but defiant Jersey Devil disappeared into the night, etching this encounter into the annals of folklore.

Strangely, there exists a theory that links the legend of the Jersey Devil to the discovery of a Hadrosaurus foulkii skeleton in Haddonfield in 1858. This nearly complete dinosaur skeleton, the first of its kind ever found, might have ignited the imaginations of locals, contributing to the creation of the Jersey Devil myth. To those unfamiliar with dinosaur anatomy, the Hadrosaurus's skeletal remains might have appeared monstrous and otherworldly.

Despite the passage of time, the legend of the Haddonfield dinosaur, which may have given birth to the Jersey Devil, remains an integral part of the state's identity, preserved and celebrated at the Academy of Natural Sciences of Drexel University in Philadelphia, Pennsylvania.

Over the centuries, the mystique of the Jersey Devil has endured, becoming an integral part of New Jersey's cultural identity. Whether a myth or a reality, it has found its way into literature, art, and popular media, making it one of the most iconic urban legends in American history.

The Bowie Goatman

In the fall of 1971, in the quiet town of Bowie, Maryland, roughly twenty miles northeast of Washington D.C., a series of unsettling events unfolded, and the small community found itself thrust into the throes of an eerie mystery. As the leaves started to change, dogs started inexplicably disappearing.

The unsettling incidents began to unfold when a young man named William Gheen was walking near the woods in early November. As he wandered through the crisp autumn air, his attention was drawn to something dark lying in the grass. Approaching cautiously, he discovered the severed head of his friend's missing dog. A chill ran down his spine as he realized that something peculiar was happening in Bowie.

Concerned residents, alarmed by the increasing number of missing dogs, urged the police to get involved. Authorities, in an attempt to quell the rising unease, attributed the beheading to a tragic accident. They claimed that the unfortunate canine had wandered along the nearby railroad tracks and was killed in a collision with a speeding locomotive. However, the teenagers in the area had a different explanation — they spoke of a mysterious creature known as the "Goatman," said to reside in the woods.

As the story gained traction in local newspapers, older residents came forward, sharing tales passed down through generations about the legendary Goatman. According to the legend, Goatman was once a scientist conducting experiments on goats at the National Agricultural Research Center in Washington D. C. In a bizarre twist of fate, he became infected with sheep DNA during an experiment that had gone awry. As his body underwent a gradual transformation into a hybrid of man and sheep, he fled to the woods. Unable to live in society, Goatman began feasting on dogs and other small animals from farms nearby.

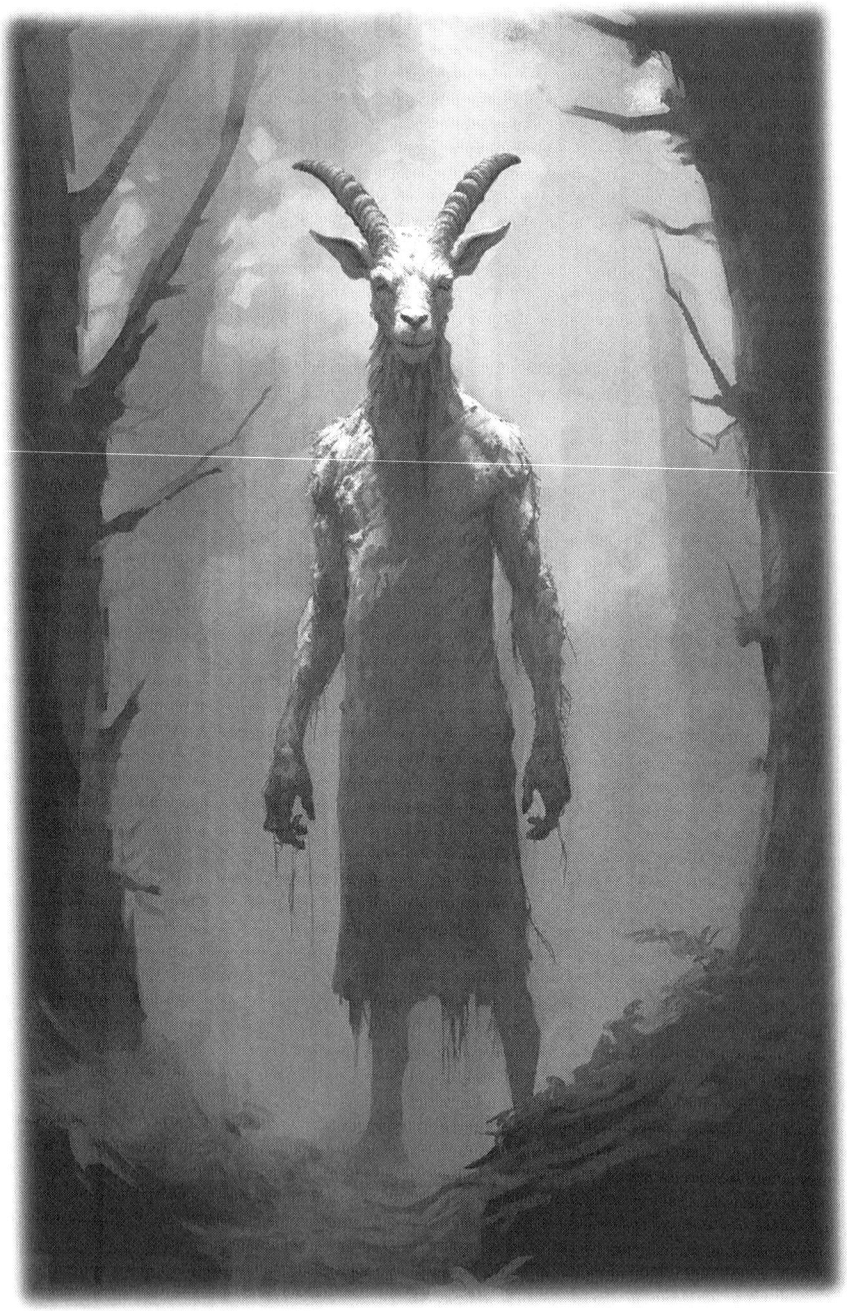

Descriptions of the Goatman varied, but a common belief held that the creature stood at around six feet tall, possessing a hairy, goat-like body. The legend grew more intricate as the years passed, with residents recounting their encounters with the elusive half-man, half-beast.

Teenagers, intrigued and perhaps driven by a sense of adventure, embarked on nighttime expeditions into the woods, hoping to catch a glimpse of the mysterious Goatman. Despite their efforts, the creature remained elusive, leaving only whispers of its presence in the rustling leaves and moonlit shadows.

As decades passed, the Goatman sightings dwindled. The once-terrifying legend transformed into a rite of passage for younger residents, a tale to be shared around campfires and passed down to the next generation.

Bowie, Maryland, may have returned to normal, but Goatman, with its haunting legacy, has forever etched itself into the town's folklore.

Creatures of the Southeast

The Lizard Man of Bishopville

In Bishopville, South Carolina, an eerie legend has fascinated locals for generations. This haunting tale revolves around the mysterious creature known as the "Lizard Man of Bishopville."

The legend traces its origins back to the summer of 1988 when a local teenager, Christopher Davis, claimed to have encountered a monstrous, scaly creature while changing a flat tire on a desolate stretch of road. Davis, a strapping young man, found himself frozen in terror as the creature emerged from the shadowy underbrush. Its eyes glowed a menacing red, and its scaly skin glistened in the moonlight.

Desperately trying to flee, Davis jumped into his car, but the creature was ruthless. It pursued him relentlessly, clawing at the vehicle's roof as he sped away. Miraculously, Davis managed to escape, but the traumatic encounter left him scarred for life.

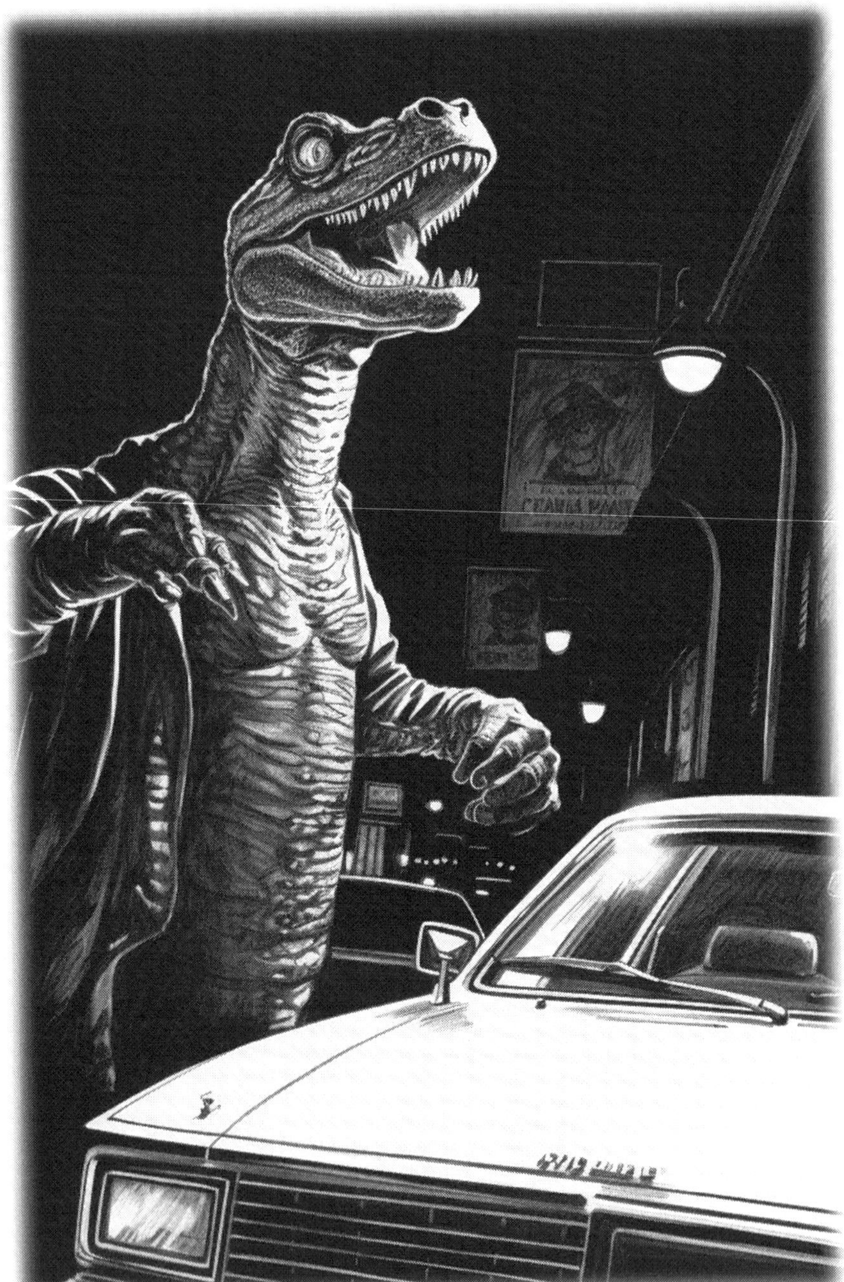

News of the Lizard Man's existence quickly spread throughout Bishopville, and the small town was soon thrust into the national spotlight. The media frenzy drew countless curious visitors, amateur monster hunters, and skeptics alike, all hoping to catch a glimpse of the elusive creature.

Local law enforcement took the matter seriously, conducting investigations and interviewing eyewitnesses. Some claimed to have seen strange tracks near the scene, while others reported missing livestock and unexplained disturbances. The mystery only deepened as reports of sightings continued to pour in.

Numerous theories about the Lizard Man's origins and motives circulated. Some believed it to be an alien creature, while others thought it might be a government experiment gone wrong. Skeptics dismissed the sightings as mere hoaxes or hallucinations, but the terror felt by those who encountered the creature was undeniably real.

Bishopville, once a quiet, unassuming town, is now forever linked to the eerie tale of its scaly, red-eyed resident.

The Cedar Key Devil Fish

In 1903, Cedar Key, Florida, found itself cast in an eerie maritime mystery that would haunt and bewilder locals for years to come. One day five veteran fishermen were walking the sandy shoreline when a scene of otherworldly proportions materialized before their eyes – a monstrous, forty-foot-long whale. Yet, it was not merely the creature's colossal size that left them in unnerved; it bore scars and markings, battle-worn gashes of some titanic struggle beneath the ocean's depths.

Exactly one month later, the same group of fishermen went about their day, oblivious to the uncanny encounter awaiting them. As their boat glided over the still waters, their eyes saw an otherworldly sea creature, gracefully ascending from the abyss and silently tailing their boats.

It was a being that defied all comprehension, an embodiment of the unknown and unseen power. Fueled by a mixture of courage and curiosity, the fishermen resolved to confront and capture this gargantuan sea monster that stalked their boats. What ensued was a cataclysmic struggle of epic proportions.

With unshaking precision, they launched a harpoon, its tip piercing the creature's massive back. Chaos ensued as the behemoth lashed out and nearly capsized one of the boats. Desperation overtook the fishermen as they fought to regain control, all the while being dragged mercilessly miles from the shore.

In an eerie twist of fate, a large steamboat appeared on the horizon, helmed by a captain who noticed the chaos. The rescue began as harpoons were unleashed, and, at last, the colossal sea monster was subdued. With their harpoon line firmly tethered to the steamboat, the beleaguered fishermen were finally safe.

The leviathan was towed back to Cedar Key's shores, where it continued to bewitch and baffle the entire community. Measuring a staggering thirty feet in length, its immense fins stretched nine feet, and it weighed an unbelievable two tons. Despite the community's tireless efforts to unravel the mystery of this cryptic sea creature, its true identity remained shrouded in eerie uncertainty.

Amidst a sea of conjecture and unease, the townspeople embraced a name for the enigmatic entity: "The Devil Fish."

The Wolf Woman of Mobile

In early April 1971, the residents of the Mobile, Alabama suburbs of Port City and Plateau found themselves in the grip of fear and fascination as they had encounters with a strange and bizarre creature that would come to be known as the "Wolf Woman of Mobile."

It all began with a series of eerie sightings that sent shockwaves through the community. The creature, described as a peculiar hybrid of a wolf and a woman, sent shivers down the spines of those who crossed its path. The top half was that of a woman, while the bottom half resembled a wolf.

The initial reports were so unsettling that many locals started calling The Press-Register, Mobile's newspaper, to report their encounters. On April 8, 1971, the newspaper decided to take the phenomenon seriously and published an article on the matter. They even included a drawing of the creature, brought to life by a newspaper illustrator, further fueling the public's intrigue.

Witnesses were eager to share their experiences with the bizarre being. They used phrases like "pretty and hairy" to describe the creature, painting a picture of an otherworldly and unsettling entity that was both alluring and frightening. One teenager was quoted as saying that their father had a run-in with the creature in a marsh, and it chased him home. The fear was so intense that the teenager's mother had resorted to keeping all the doors and windows locked.

Rumors circulated that the creature had possibly escaped from a circus sideshow, adding another layer of mystery to the story. The entire community was on edge, and even the police couldn't ignore the flood of reports pouring in. While the police refrained from making official statements, they couldn't ignore the sheer volume of sightings and launched an investigation to ascertain the nature of this phenomenon.

Sightings of beings that were part-human and part-wolf have long been part of folklore and legends. The most common association being the werewolf, a creature that has terrified imaginations for centuries. It's worth noting that such legends have their roots in American Indian folklore and have always been a source of fascination and dread.

However, after little more than ten days, the Wolf Woman of Mobile Alabama mysteriously disappeared, never to be seen again. The newspaper, in an article dated shortly after the initial reports, referred to the creature as an "apparition" and a "phantom." The true nature of this enigmatic being remained a puzzle. Was it a supernatural entity, or perhaps, a feral woman raised by wolves? Maybe it was just a prank. The mystery, whatever it may be, left an indelible mark on the city of Mobile, Alabama during those first two weeks of April 1971.

The Poligny Werewolves and the Rougarou

In the annals of dark history, the Poligny Werewolves stand out as figures of gruesome notoriety. Their harrowing story began in 1521, a time when superstition and fear of the supernatural were rampant, and tales of witchcraft and lycanthropy could lead to brutal consequences.

The stage for this macabre tale was set in Besançon, France, when the self-confessed werewolf, Michel Verdun, and his accomplice, Pierre Burgot, were brought to trial by Inquisitor Jean Boin. The origins of their infamy lie in an encounter with a traveler who was passing through the area. This traveler faced a terrifying ordeal when he was suddenly attacked by a ferocious wolf. Remarkably, he managed to fend off the beast, wounding it and forcing it to retreat. What happened is almost unbelievable.

Following the bloodied trail left by the injured creature, the traveler stumbled upon a desolate hut. Inside, he encountered a local named Michel Verdun, who was under the care of his wife for bloody wounds on his body. The traveler's instincts kicked in, suspecting that Verdun's injury might be connected to the vicious wolf attack he had just endured. It was this suspicion that would unleash a torrent of dreadful events. Michel Verdun was swiftly apprehended and subjected to the excruciating tortures of the Inquisition. Under the unimaginable pain and duress, he confessed to being a shapeshifter, revealing a tale that would shock and terrify.

Verdun's confession went beyond mere lycanthropy; he disclosed his involvement in diabolism, murder, and the cannibalistic consumption of human flesh. Furthermore, he named his two equally malevolent accomplices: Pierre Burgot and another man named Moyset, who served the devil himself.

Their dreadful journey into the world of the supernatural began when Burgot encountered Moyset, who made enticing promises of protection, wealth, and the retrieval of Burgot's lost sheep. In return, Moyset demanded unwavering allegiance and a renunciation of Christianity. Burgot accepted, marking the beginning of his nightmarish pact.

Burgot delved into a shadowy existence, serving the devil for two years as his flock of sheep remained inexplicably unharmed. His involvement in diabolical ceremonies saw him transform into a werewolf alongside Verdun. According to their accounts, they would strip naked, apply a salve provided by their sinister masters, and feel themselves metamorphosing into wolves.

In their lupine forms, they roamed the night with unnatural swiftness and savagery, carrying out a string of horrifying atrocities. Their gruesome acts included the murder and consumption of children, women, and even animals. They painted a horrific scene of terror and violence that defied the boundaries of human morality.

As swiftly as their dark reign began, it ended in a chilling climax. The Inquisitor's judgment was swift and unrelenting. The Poligny Werewolves were promptly sentenced to execution for their heinous crimes, bringing a gruesome but fitting end to this tale of terror and transformation.

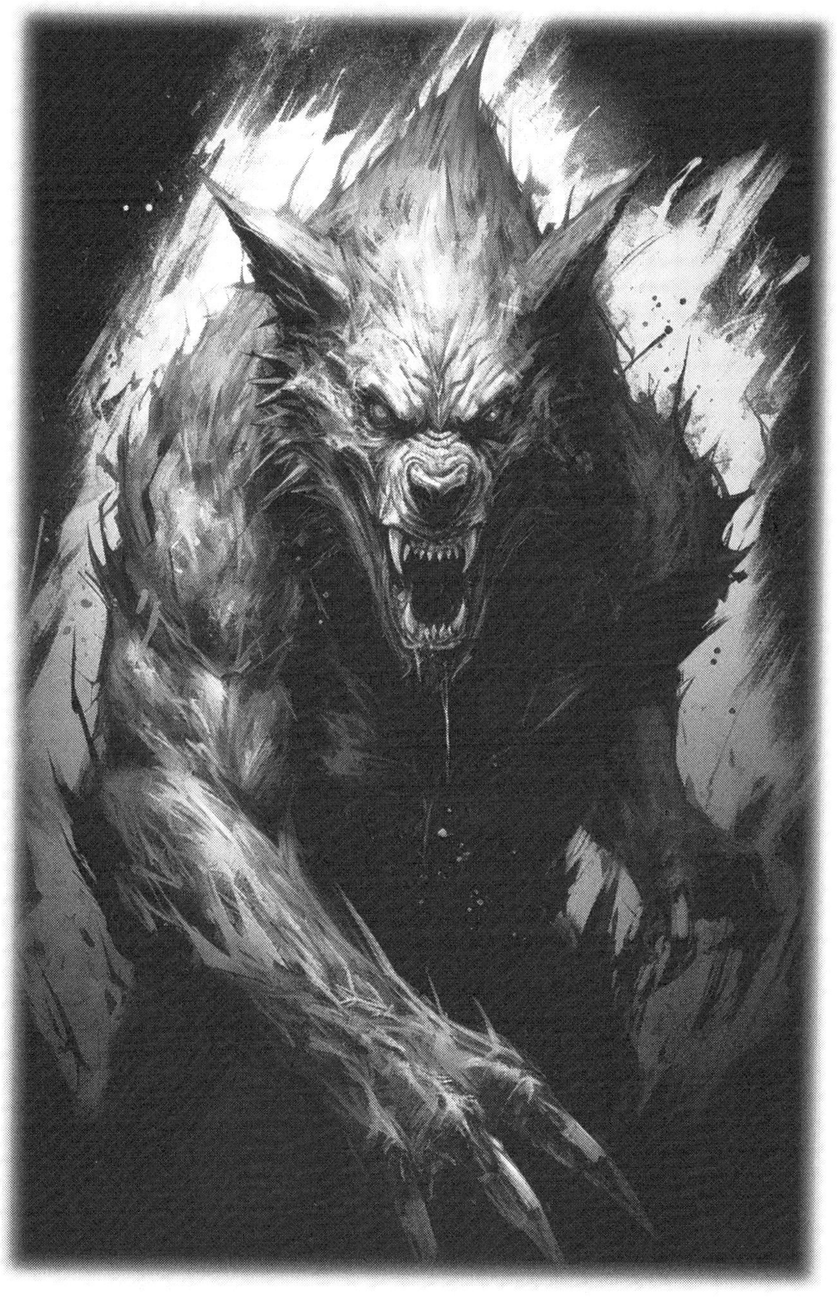

The Birth of the Rougarou

Deep in the heart of the swamps surrounding New Orleans, a chilling legend lurked—an entity known as the Rougarou. This creature, a blend of ancient folklore and local superstitions, was both feared and whispered about by generations of Louisianians. The tale of the Rougarou originated centuries earlier, intertwining history, culture, and the mysterious forces of the bayou.

The story of the Rougarou began with the settlers who arrived in Louisiana from France. These colonists brought with them a rich tapestry of traditions and beliefs, including the legend of the "loup-garou," a term originating from the French words "loup" (wolf) and "garou" (man-wolf). Over time, the tale was adopted and transformed by the unique cultural blend that emerged in the region.

According to local lore, the Rougarou was once a man like the Poligy werewolves who had strayed from the path of righteousness and embraced wickedness. In some versions, he had committed a grave sin. Regardless of the reason, the man's transgressions led to a curse, transforming him into the monstrous Rougarou.

The transformation from man to beast was not a one-time event. The legend often spoke of a curse that could be passed down through generations, afflicting those who carried the bloodline tainted by the Rougarou's curse. The curse was said to be activated under specific circumstances, such as failing to attend Mass for seven consecutive years or breaking religious customs during Lent. The curse could also be transferred to a new victim if the Rougarou drew blood from them.

The Rougarou was said to be a fearsome creature, a blend of human and animal traits. Its form varied in the retelling of the legend, but some common attributes emerged — a tall, hairy creature with the head of a wolf or dog, sharp claws, and glowing red eyes. It possessed incredible strength and was known to have a sinister hunger for human flesh.

In the dead of night, when the moon cast an eerie glow over the swamps, the Rougarou would emerge from its hidden lair. It prowled through the darkness, stalking its prey and striking fear into the hearts of those who heard its eerie howls echoing through the bayou. The Rougarou was a creature of both myth and reality, a manifestation of the fears and uncertainties that permeated the Cajun culture.

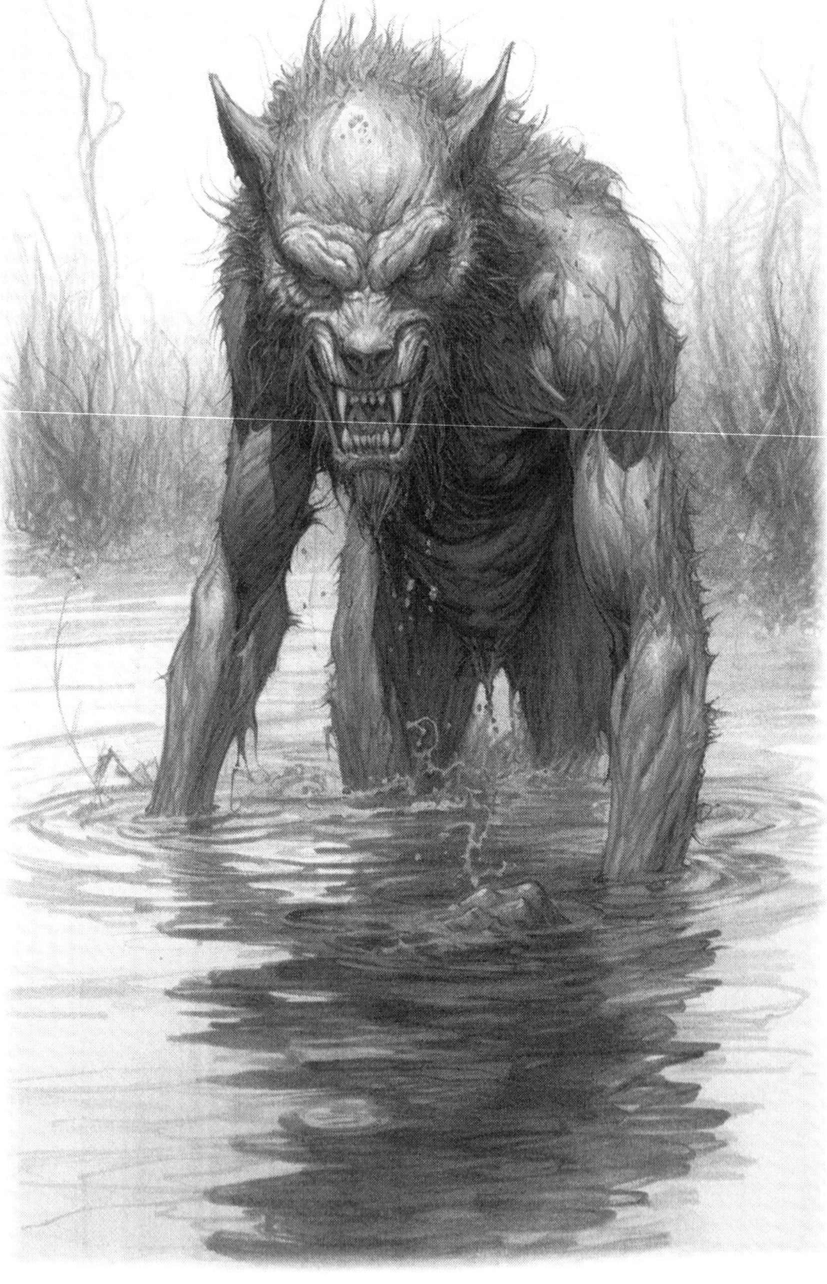

The legend of the Rougarou served multiple purposes within Cajun culture. It served as a cautionary tale, warning against the consequences of immoral behavior and the importance of adhering to religious customs. Parents used the story to keep their children in line, ensuring they attended Mass and maintained good behavior. The Rougarou also played a role in preserving Cajun traditions, passing down stories from one generation to the next.

This eerie tale of two distinct but interconnected legends — the Poligny Werewolves and the Rougarou — illustrates how folklore evolves and adapts to different cultural landscapes and historical contexts.

The Mississippi River Monster

In the summer of 1877 an unsettling story began to circulate among riverboat crews up and down the Mississippi River. This chilling tale spoke of a peculiar and colossal creature lurking in the river's depths, an entity that would defy explanation and captivate the imaginations of all who dared to venture near the water.

The accounts of those who encountered this aquatic behemoth described a creature around 20 feet in length. The Mississippi River, once regarded as a lifeline for transportation and commerce, had now become tinged with an element of danger and uncertainty.

This aquatic anomaly was not content with remaining hidden beneath the water's surface. On multiple occasions, the riverboat crews would be subject to a bone-chilling spectacle: the leviathan would emerge from the murky depths to prey upon the horses and cattle daring to cross the river. With a calculated and eerie grace, the creature would strike, devastating any unfortunate livestock in its path.

The climax of this unsettling series of events occurred on September 19, 1877, in New Madrid, Missouri. A seemingly routine ferry crossing soon turned into a nightmarish ordeal. The ferry, laden with two wagons and carrying three men, suddenly found itself in the midst of a violent maelstrom.

Out of nowhere, the water surrounding the ferry erupted into chaos. The passengers were thrown into a frenzy as the creature, true to its dreadful reputation, rammed the vessel with its large head. The violent impact sent the ferry lurching wildly, threatening to capsize at any moment. One of the passengers was flung into the river, left to grapple with the turbulent currents and the sinister presence lurking beneath.

But the creature's assault did not end there. As it released the ferry, it swam away, leaving large waves in its wake. The ferocity of its tail's motion created waves several feet high.

The most astonishing moment of this nightmarish crossing was still to come. The creature, now about forty feet away, unleashed a mesmerizing display of power and malevolence. It propelled a towering jet of water, ten feet high, from the river's surface. The spectacle was punctuated by a spine-tingling shriek, a sound that echoed across the waters and resonated with the primal fear that had gripped everyone who bore witness to the terror.

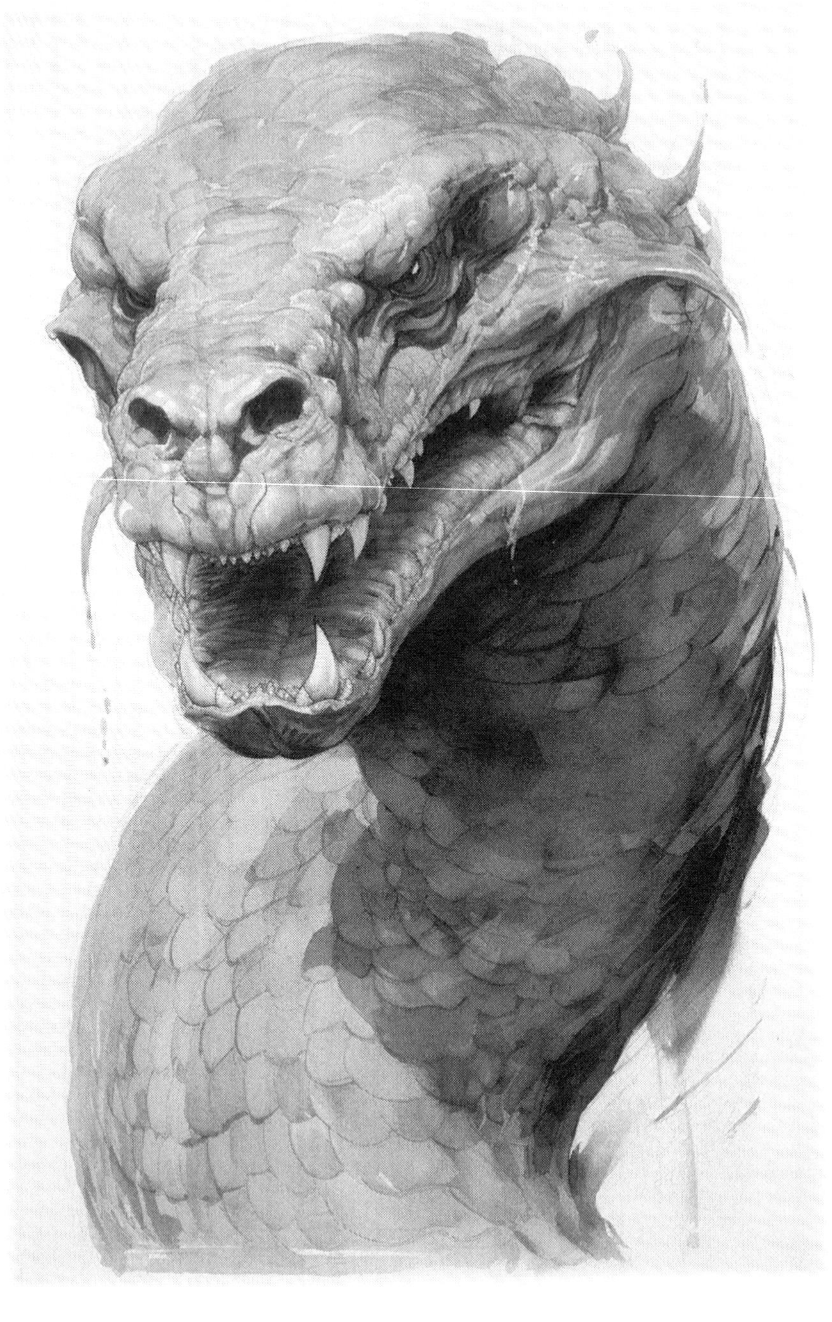

Then, just as abruptly as it had appeared, the creature vanished. It plunged back into the dark waters, leaving behind a shaken and bewildered group of passengers. With sheer determination and frantic effort, the men managed to steer their damaged ferry to safety along the shore.

While the passengers on the New Madrid ferry escaped with their lives, other parts of the Mississippi River witnessed more encounters with the river monster. In October 1877, a towboat captain towing barges faced a menacing and surreal confrontation fifteen miles north of Memphis, Tennessee. As he was about to pull into port, the towboat captain's vessel bumped into something in the water, jolting the boat. He was not prepared for what he saw when he peered into the water, initially mistaking it for an uprooted tree. However, as he observed more closely, it became evident that it was a massive, thirty-foot-long river monster swiftly gliding towards him.

A harrowing confrontation ensued as the creature attacked the barge. It rammed the vessel, causing chaos and panic among the crew. The violent encounter led to some of the crew members falling overboard, while the detached barges floated down the river. Tragically, one sailor drowned when a barge was completely capsized by the monstrous entity. The next day, another unsettling encounter occurred when a flatboat carrying a man and his two horses was attacked in Mississippi. The creature targeted the horses, completely devouring them.

News of these horrifying encounters spread rapidly along the Mississippi River, with numerous people coming forward to share their own stories of seeing the river monster. Among them was Jabez Smith, a farmer from Cahokia, Illinois, who recounted a disturbing incident that happened to his son. His son had been working on the farm when he heard a terrifying roar coming from the woods, unlike any sound he had ever heard. Fearing for his life, he watched in shock as a serpent-like creature with a large mouth full of fangs and a mane of reddish hair emerged from the forest. The creature appeared to fixate on a bull inside a pen and viciously attacked it. A brutal battle ensued, but just when it seemed that the bull might prevail, the serpent let out a cry, unfurled wings from its sides, and took flight, resembling a monstrous bat. It soared through the air before descending into the river with a thunderous splash. The surreal event left those who heard it bewildered and fascinated.

News of this extraordinary account reached the ears of a St. Louis Republican reporter, who felt compelled to visit Jabez Smith and investigate the story. Following the reporter's visit, a local professor examined the bull and noted the extensive marks on its body, indicative of a fierce struggle.

On January 8, 1878, an event unfolded along the Mississippi River that would add another chapter to the legend of the river's monster. John Davidson, the captain of the steamboat Silver Moon, found himself at the wharf in Lawrenceburg, Indiana.

As Captain Davidson observed the surroundings, his attention was seized by an unusual sight. What he initially mistook for a floating log quickly revealed itself to be something far more astonishing. In the water before him, a monstrous creature lifted its head, its features more surreal than any creature of this earth. Its form boasted a large mouth and a slimy, reddish mane that adorned its serpentine body. The creature's length extended to approximately thirty feet, and its menacing presence defied conventional explanation.

Upon witnessing this grotesque and surreal sight, Captain Davidson reacted swiftly. He called out to his first mate, urging him to come and witness this inexplicable monster. However, as he did so, the creature abruptly went under, vanishing below the water's surface with an eerie grace. Left in the wake of the creature's passage, Captain Davidson was seized by a sense of awe and trepidation. He understood the magnitude of what he had seen and felt compelled to share his account.

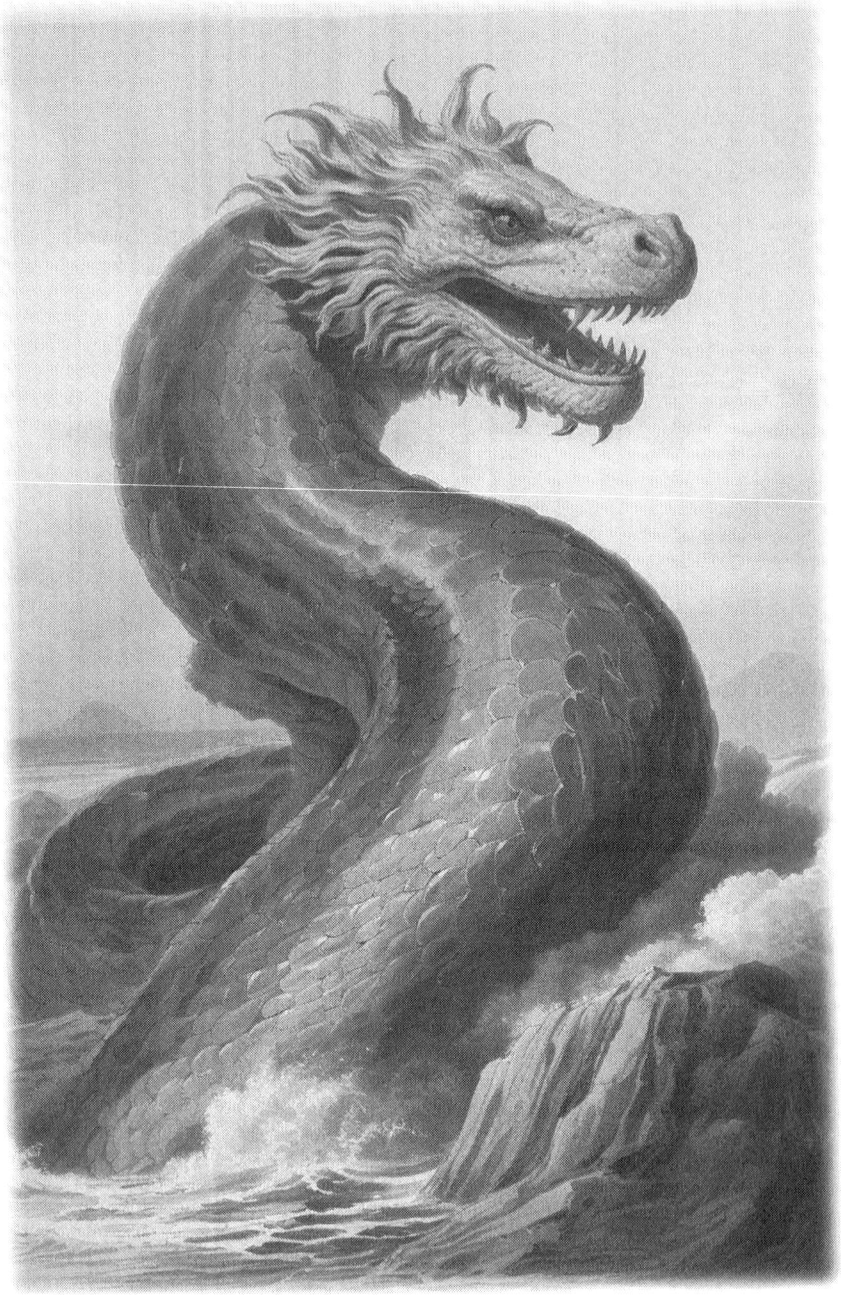

After the encounter, Captain Davidson wrote a letter to a Cincinnati newspaper, imploring those who plied their trade along the Mississippi River to exercise caution and vigilance. His words contained a warning, a call for action, and a plea for vigilance in the face of an entity that defied reason and explanation.

As the tale of the Mississippi River Monster spread, accounts from various regions continued to emerge, further fueling the fear and fascination surrounding the creature. Yet, just as mysteriously as it had appeared, the river monster vanished, leaving behind a sense of wonder and trepidation. Veteran riverboat men, their faces etched with the wisdom of the river, passed down the tale to the rookies, ensuring that the chilling story of the Mississippi's monstrous serpent would endure.

The Tennessee River Monster

In the 1800s, the Cherokee spoke of a chilling legend about a monstrous creature lurking in the Tennessee River. The creature was a twenty-five-foot-long terror with a dog-like head and a towering two-foot tailfin. It was believed to be swift, leaving victims with no chance to react, its giant teeth sealing their fate, leaving few survivors. It was rumored to hibernate for extended periods.

Buck Sutton's sighting in 1822 marked the first recorded encounter. Billy Burns' sighting five years added to the accounts, describing a creature with a yellow belly and a blue-black back. Strange coincidences surrounded the sightings as both Sutton and Burns died within days of their encounters. In 1829, Jim Windom had an eerie but unthreatening encounter, coming face-to-face with the creature on the banks of the river. However, he and his wife, Sallie, survived to tell the tale.

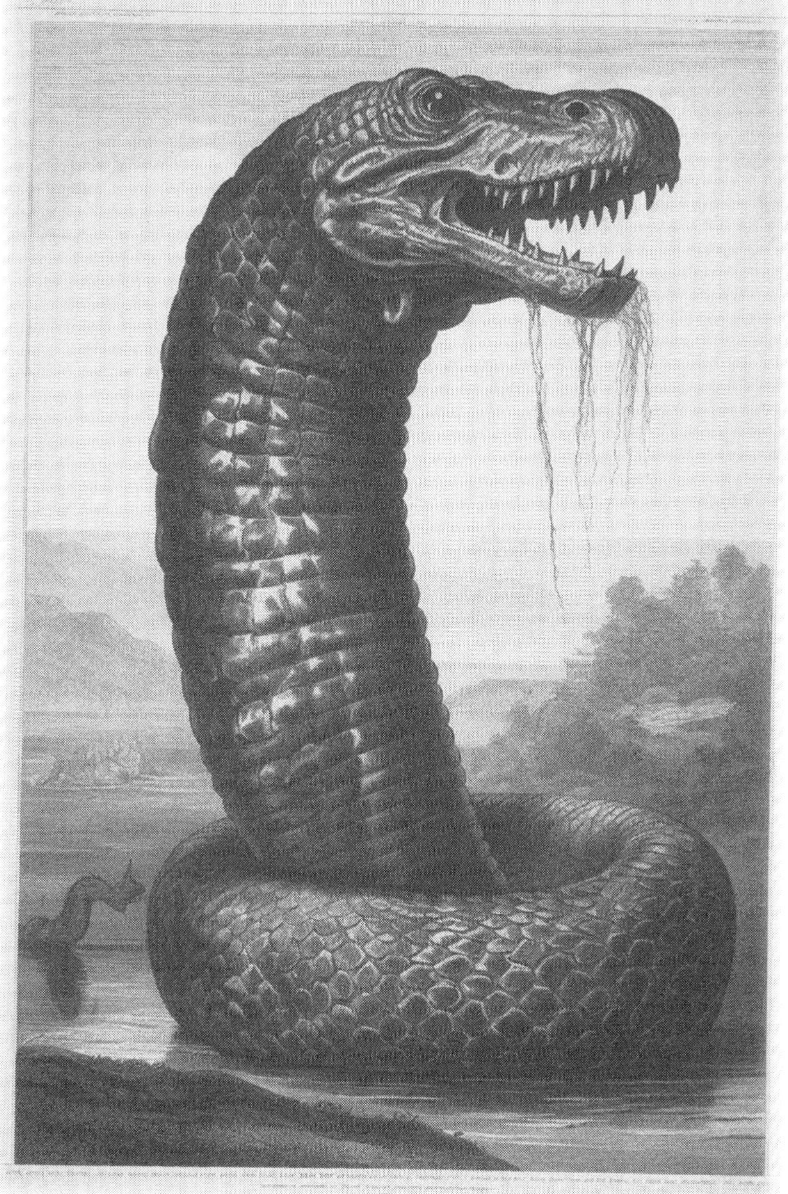

More reports followed, but with an unconventional pattern. In 1836, some individuals saw the creature but managed to escape, suggesting that the monster had aged, losing its once incredible speed. The final recorded encounter happened in 1839 when J. C. Wilson witnessed the beast near Chickamauga Island, deciding wisely to retreat.

Theories abounded regarding the Tennessee River Monster's origin and fate. Some believed steamboats frightened it away, while others thought it migrated to different waters. Skeptics dismissed the tales as folklore created to dissuade children from riverbanks.

However, the legend went deeper into Native American lore. According to an ancient Cherokee tale, in 1812, a native disturbed the creature in Wildcat Lake. The monster emerged, ascended into the air, glided over the mountain, and vanished into the Tennessee River near Chickamauga Creek.

Decades later, in 1913, the creature appeared near Pan Gap, observed by sawmill employees. It displayed odd behavior, swimming downstream to shallow waters to feed on small fish before hiding in deeper waters near the mill. Witnesses described a horse-like head with a long neck and rubbery black skin.

Nevertheless, skeptics dismissed the tales as mere folklore, concocted by river dwellers to dissuade their children from wandering too close to the riverbanks.

The Stench

In the late 1920s, in the small town of Red Boiling Springs, Tennessee, the tranquility of a moonlit evening was disrupted by an event that would be remembered by Pamela Meador and her family for generations.

The evening was calm, and Pamela was on her way home, walking down a winding road that led through the woods. An eccentric old man lived in the area so when she heard eerie sounds emanating from the woods she chalked it up to the old recluse and continued walking.

However, as Pamela continued down the desolate road, a disconcerting feeling crept over her. It was as if unseen eyes bore into her back, and inexplicable fear clung to her like a ghostly veil. The young girl turned, her heart pounding, expecting to catch the odd codger in some playful or eerie prank. What Pamela saw, though, was no man. It was a colossal, eight-foot-tall creature. It loomed ominously, resembling a Sasquatch.

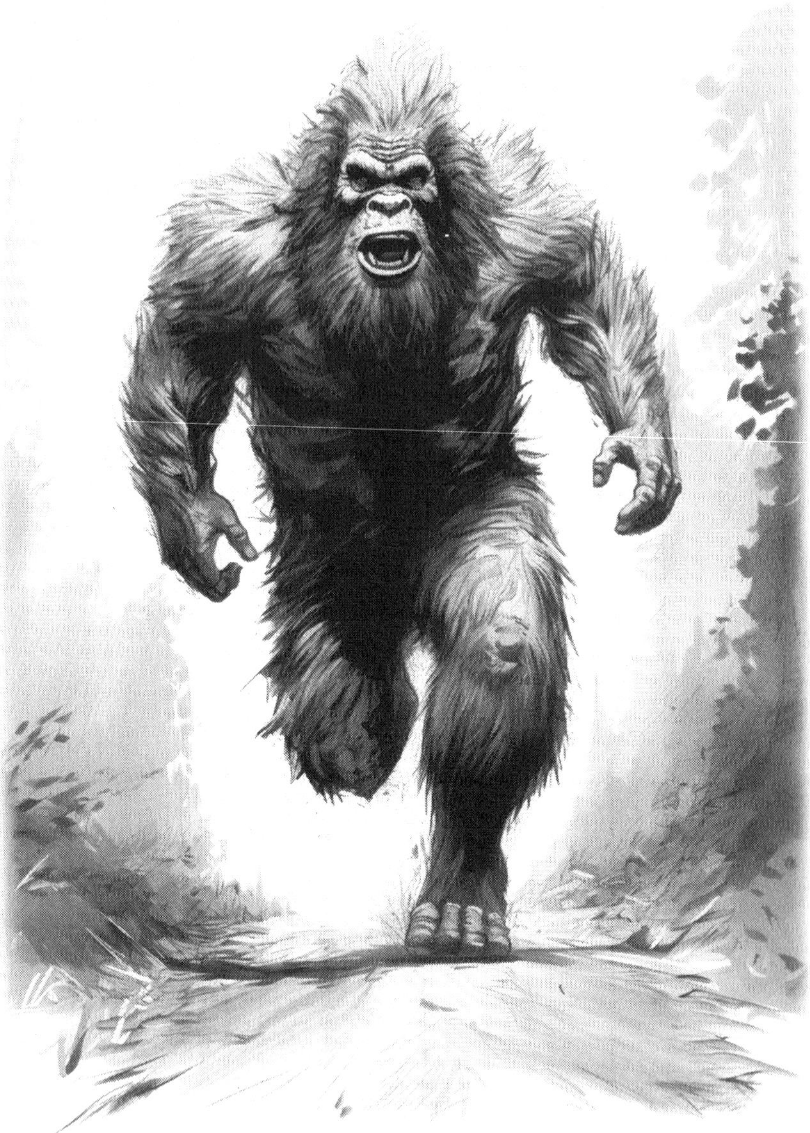

With a terror that gripped her heart, Pamela knew that she had to run. She broke into a sprint, each frantic step taking her closer to the safety of her home. Yet, what compounded her fear was not merely the towering figure in pursuit but the nauseating stench that enveloped the creature. It was a repugnant odor that seemed to taint the very air around her.

As Pamela's frantic cries echoed through the night, drawing nearer to her house, her father, emerged onto the front porch, clutching a shotgun with grim determination.

Fearful for her life, Pamela reached the porch, her voice trembling as she pleaded with her father to shoot the nightmarish creature that was relentlessly chasing her.

With his daughter's desperation etched into her tear-stricken face, her father stood ready to confront whatever nightmare lurked in the darkness. Yet, as Pamela and her father scanned the moonlit landscape, the beast vanished into the woods, leaving behind only the lingering residue of its nauseating stench.

As the years passed, Pamela recounted the harrowing tale to friends and family, each retelling steeped in the unwavering conviction of her truth. Her son, Eric Edmonds, bears witness to his mother's character, asserting that she was a God-fearing woman who never lied. "My mother didn't make things up," he avowed. "She said that story with unwavering conviction, and the one thing she was adamant about was the horrible smell of the creature as it chased her."

Monkey Woman Bridge

For those who came of age around Smyrna, Tennessee in the mid to late 20th century, the tale of the Monkey Woman that lived beneath the bridge at One Mile Lane, where it crosses Stewart's Creek, is a haunting memory. What began as a mere urban legend swiftly evolved into a vital piece of local folklore, eventually passing down through the generations.

The legend of the Monkey Woman Bridge has assumed various forms, each adding its unique twist to the unsettling tale. One of these variations spins the story of a lady living in the area during the 1800s who, unusually, had a monkey as a pet. One night, she decided to go on a moonlit horseback ride. However, the horse, spooked by something in the night, bolted into a frenzied gallop, throwing both the lady and her primate friend into the murky waters of Stewart's Creek. It was from this ill-fated incident that the half-monkey, half-woman creature is said to have emerged, forever haunting the vicinity.

Another eerie incarnation of the Monkey Woman's origins suggests that she was a deranged woman who lived in the area, or someone driven off the bridge one night during a violent storm. Some daringly proclaim that she was a witch whose vengeful curses awaited those bold enough to call out to her in the dead of night.

Naturally, it became a rite of passage for local teenagers to flirt with danger by taunting and berating the mythical entity lurking beneath the bridge. Countless young men were dared to stand upon the bridge and chant, "I hate the Monkey Woman!" ten times in a row. However, fear often stopped them at the eighth or ninth time. The braver souls who managed to complete the sinister task promptly fled the scene, never staying long enough to witness the creature manifest.

The Bay Raven of Old Douglass Cemetery

Hidden away on Old Douglas Lane in Gallatin, Tennessee, lies one of Sumner County's most ancient burial grounds—the Bay Raven Cemetery. Once named the Douglass Cemetery, this site has borne witness to burials dating back to the 1820s, where nearly two dozen souls found their final resting place in the small North Gallatin cemetery.

Bay Raven has, for decades, been a source of both fascination and trepidation for the youth of Sumner County. In the mid-20th century, it transformed into a gathering spot for high school kids seeking late-night adventures, attempting to scare one another with tales of the supernatural.

"There's something not right about that place," whispered Jean Blunkhall, a local who spent her teenage years near Bay Raven. "At night, that cemetery is one of the scariest places I've ever been in my life!"

But as the cemetery's popularity with the youth grew, so did a strange and sinister story that began to circulate around the town square. Bay Raven was harboring an unearthly secret—a monstrous entity that lurked in the shadows.

Cemeteries are often associated with ghostly tales, but at Bay Raven, it wasn't apparitions or elusive phantoms weaving in and out of the gnarled trees and crumbling tombstones. No, this cemetery sheltered a fearsome creature!

Word of this monster gradually reached Nashville and even caught the attention of The Tennessean, the local newspaper. In February 1955, the paper dispatched a reporter to Gallatin to capture a photograph of the alleged beast that roamed the cemetery under the dark of night.

Regrettably, the elusive entity was never captured on film, but the reporter did manage to interview those living nearby.

According to the article, the colossal menace bore a resemblance to a gorilla but was the size of a bull, with powerful hind legs. Its insatiable appetite led it to devour dogs, sheep, and calves from neighboring farms. In one gruesome account, a farmer awoke to a blood-soaked scene after the creature had consumed thirty-six dogs during the night, swallowing them whole but spitting out their severed feet. But the creature's predation was not confined to meat alone; it devoured a wagon full of dried apples left out overnight, leaving not a single apple untouched by morning.

Over time, the legend of Bay Raven evolved, taking on different forms. Some claimed to have seen a monstrous being, a grotesque hybrid of man and raven, lurking in the shadows of the cemetery. Another version of the story tells that circling one of the trees in the graveyard three times would summon a giant raven, which would circle overhead, meeting you in the middle of the cemetery.

Sadly, the Old Douglass Cemetery has been consigned to the annals of time, with many graves vandalized or robbed. Several final resting places have been disturbed, and the remains are no longer at peace within this unsettling, forgotten burial ground.

The Hendersonville Shadow

Behind the Windridge Condos on Edgewood Drive in Hendersonville, Tennessee is a large, wooded area. According to those that grew up nearby, it is the epicenter for something very dark.

"When you go down to Dana and Woodyside, there is a dead end," explained Aaron Brewster. "They say it was owned by an Indian named Lee.

One night, around 8:30 or so, we were hanging out in front of my buddy's house. As we were standing there, we heard a rattle in the trees next to us. Then we heard a whooping sound. It was a creature, but I didn't know what it was."

Curious as to what was causing the commotion, Aaron took off after it. But when he got back into the woods, he couldn't find it, but he did hear it.

"When I got back there, I heard a very high pitch squeal," continued Aaron. "It was long and drawn out. The messed-up part was that it had three octaves on top of it. There was a high pitch, with a low pitch under it then it had a mid-range. It was like three things making the same noise.

Keep in mind it is pitch black outside and we start going deeper and deeper into the woods. I started to hear limbs breaking above us. I looked up but didn't see anything. I could hear it and I could see the limbs falling. As this was happening, my buddy got scared and took off.

I kept walking and I saw a straight shadow about three feet tall moving through the trees. It moved like a monkey, but it didn't make any sense because there are no monkeys in that part of Tennessee."

After the strange encounter Aaron started researching what could be in the area or make such an incredible sound. To his surprise, there are apes that can produce a similar noise.

"It was like someone had one of those apes as a pet and it got out," said Aaron. "I don't know if it's paranormal, but if it is, it seemed more Indian than paranormal."

But that wasn't the only time Aaron had an encounter in the area.

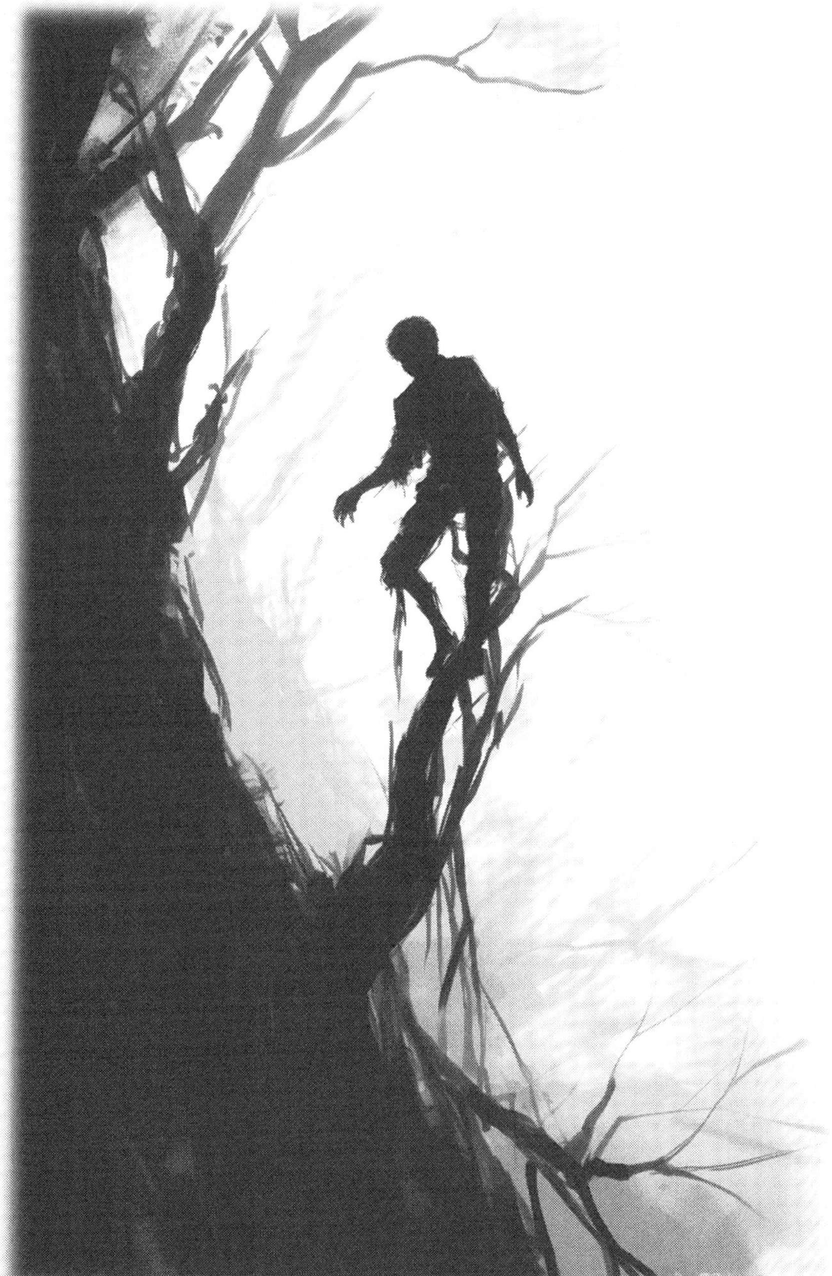

"When I was 14, I was walking down Dana and at the dead end was a tree," explained Aaron. "I saw a black thing about five or six feet tall with no face or features. It had black steam coming off his face and it was standing on a limb. All I could think was, 'There's no way that a man is standing on that limb because it was too thin. He was standing about 20 or 25 feet up. I locked onto it, and I locked up and then started to shake. I finally broke away and looked back and it was gone!"

The Knoxville Wampus Cat

In late January 1932, Ike Payne, a hardworking farmer living on the outskirts of Knoxville, Tennessee, experienced a series of mysterious and unsettling events. One particularly chilly and dark night, Ike was abruptly awakened by a commotion coming from his chicken coop situated behind his farmhouse. Startled and alarmed, he instinctively grabbed his revolver and rushed outside into the darkness to investigate the disturbance.

As he reached the chicken coop, he was met with a perplexing sight. In the dim moonlight, he could discern a creature that, to his horror, appeared to be a large wolf with a pair of menacing yellow eyes, each the size of half dollars, and a long, bushy tail that seemed to dance eerily in the darkness. Fearing for his livelihood and the safety of his chickens, Ike Payne did not hesitate; he raised his revolver and fired at the ferocious intruder.
The deafening gunshot was accompanied by a wild, unearthly screech that sent shivers down Ike's spine, reminiscent of a deranged wildcat. The creature, now injured, retreated into the night, disappearing into the dense woods that surrounded the Payne farm. Little did Ike know that this terrifying encounter marked the beginning of a disturbing series of events that would grip the community.

A few nights later, the creature returned to Ike's farm, its intent clear as it savagely killed some of his helpless chickens. The once tranquil countryside had been thrust into a state of fear and uncertainty by the presence of this mysterious, malevolent entity.

Around the same time, A. D. Hale, who lived on Washington Pike, was confronted by his own unsettling experiences. One night, he discovered one of his bulldogs lifeless, the victim of a brutal attack. The following evening, another of his loyal bulldogs mysteriously vanished. As neighbors began to share stories of these bizarre incidents and attributed them to the notorious "Wampus Cat," Hale vehemently dismissed the claims. He insisted that his bulldogs had fallen prey to a large, rabid German Shepherd or some other equally large, mad dog.

However, as more reports of strange encounters began to surface in the community, skepticism waned. Policeman John Jenkins, who lived nearby, endured his own encounter with the mysterious creature when it attacked his puppies. Two of them tragically lost their lives, while the third was left seriously injured. Jenkins' wife offered a detailed description of the assailant, describing a creature standing around two feet tall with yellow eyes and a bushy tail, appearing more foxlike than feline.

News of these mysterious events quickly spread throughout the region. On February 9, 1932, the headline "Is There Another Wampus Roaming About the City?" graced the front page of the Knoxville Journal. The legend of a mythical creature, similar to a panther, that had long been rumored to roam East Tennessee, had rekindled public interest. This creature was believed to terrorize local farms, attacking small animals with apparent pleasure, yet never consuming its victims. According to one eyewitness, who happened to be a railroad employee, the Wampus Cat was a colossal beast, almost as large as one of the train cars.

While some remained skeptical, George Bell's dog, "Tip," became another victim of the elusive entity in February 1932. With unmistakable bite marks on the canine's neck and hind leg, Bell was convinced that a ferocious Wampus Cat was responsible for the attack. He shared this belief with reporters and was resolute in his conviction that it was not a coyote or any other escapee from a circus, but indeed a Wampus Cat.

After a series of attacks in 1932, the Wampus Cat retreated into the deep woods, occasionally glimpsed by hunters. However, the creature returned in September 1937, once again plaguing the residents of Washington Pike. It broke into R. J. Duncan's home under the cover of night, claiming the lives of two pet baby rabbits. It also invaded Ed Acuff's farm, where it mercilessly slaughtered 13 chickens. Dr. N. A. Williamson, a local dentist, awoke one fateful morning to a gruesome sight: his chicken coops had been shredded, the wire netting torn to shreds by powerful jaws. Even the 2x4s used to construct the coop were found chewed into pieces. The massacre left 24 dead chickens, with only one surviving the onslaught. Curiously, the Wampus Cat showed no interest in consuming its victims.

Meanwhile, Fred Edmonds, Williamson's neighbor, reported a disturbing incident involving his hound dogs, which howled and whimpered in abject fear around 3 a.m. It was clear that the Wampus Cat had left a lasting impression on these animals. In another distressing event, W. T. Acuff's large collie returned home, bearing deep scratches, wounds, and profuse bleeding. A local veterinarian, Dr. Queener, who examined the injured dog, concluded that the creature responsible was far from being a mere possum.

In early October 1937, A. B. Cunningham found himself in a terrifying encounter as the Wampus Cat attacked his chicken coop, leaving five chickens dead in its wake before vanishing into the night. Desperate to capture the elusive creature, a neighbor brought over bloodhounds, but they proved unsuccessful in picking up the scent of the menacing entity.

Several days later, William Tibbs, a local hunter, embarked on what he called a "big booger hunt," believing that the creature responsible for the chicken massacres was nothing more than an 18-pound possum he had previously seen in the area. The hunt quickly escalated, with Tibbs, his three hunting dogs, and a staggering 70 volunteers, some with their own pack of hounds, scouring the area in a fervent pursuit of the mysterious Wampus Cat. The turnout was so substantial that Dr. Williamson humorously remarked to a reporter that he might consider opening a hamburger stand on his property to make a few bucks from the assembled crowd.

Yet, even as the search party scoured the woods, the elusive Wampus Cat made a deadly appearance at Claude Webb's home. It attacked one of his hogs, which squealed in agony, and when two of Webb's dogs, a bulldog and a German shepherd, courageously confronted the creature, they were effortlessly repelled.

The Wampus Cat fled into the night as Webb raced outside, brandishing his shotgun. According to Webb, the creature resembled a cat in some respects but was roughly the size of a medium-sized dog.

Later that same night, Jack Walker, a local resident, reported another sighting. As the creature crossed North Broadway near Branson Avenue, an approaching automobile forced it to make an astonishing 10-foot leap into the woods, evading a potential collision.

Policeman George Paker, however, held a unique perspective on the matter. He asserted that the Wampus Cat was not a cat at all, having personally observed seven large possums while on patrol one night near Washington Pike. He surmised that these possums, acting in tandem, were the culprits behind the chaos, responsible for killing dogs and terrorizing farm animals.

In early November, a group of three men were hunting along the Tennessee River when their hunting dogs started barking frenziedly. As one of the dogs approached a patch of tall grass, it was pounced upon by a lightning-fast creature. Though wounded, the dog managed to escape. The hunters shot the assailant and brought in a veterinarian to identify the creature. When they returned, the vet dismissed the fears and laughter ensued as the assailant was nothing more than an ordinary house cat. However, the Wampus Cat had not been vanquished; by the year's end, it had claimed the lives of over a hundred chickens in the area.

The Wampus Cat temporarily withdrew from the limelight, only to resurface in February 1939. This time, it targeted the Acuff family farm again, ruthlessly killing seven hens and one rooster. The beast, as before, tore through the wire netting and launched a violent attack on the helpless chickens. A hunting party formed to track down the elusive creature, but their efforts proved futile.

Following early 1939, reports of the Wampus Cat's presence ceased in Knoxville, Tennessee. However, this didn't signify its end, as reports of sightings and attacks surfaced in other regions, including Oklahoma and Texas, suggesting that the legendary and elusive creature had merely moved on, leaving behind a legacy of fear and mystery.

The Hopkinsville Goblins

In the small, quiet town of Hopkinsville, Kentucky, s, a strange and unsettling tale unfolded one fateful night in 1955. The Sutton family, comprised of eight adults and three children, lived in a modest farmhouse on the outskirts of the town where the event took place.

On the evening of August 21st, the Suttons gathered around their kitchen table, sharing laughter and stories after a day of work. As twilight faded into darkness, an eerie atmosphere began to envelop the household. Suddenly, a loud commotion erupted from outside, shattering the peaceful evening.

Glancing towards the window, Billy Ray Sutton, the family patriarch, caught sight of bizarre, glowing lights descending from the sky. Panic set in as the lights drew nearer, revealing strange figures that seemed to defy description.

As the Suttons locked themselves inside, the tension inside the farmhouse reached its peak. Armed with shotguns and a sense of unease, they huddled together, trying to make sense of the surreal events unfolding outside. Time seemed to stretch as the hours passed, and the strange entities made their first move.

Small, greenish creatures with oversized heads and long, spindly limbs emerged from the shadows. The Suttons were stunned by their appearance – these beings looked like something out of a science fiction tale. Fear gripped them as they realized the creatures were approaching the house, their movements quick and unnatural.

The family's fear turned to desperation as the night wore on. They fired at the creatures, but their shots seemed to have little effect. The creatures, seemingly unfazed, continued to skitter around the property. Fear soon gave way to a sense of helplessness, and the Suttons feared they were trapped in a nightmare they couldn't wake from.

But just as quickly as the chaos had erupted, the bizarre visitors suddenly retreated. The creatures vanished into the night, leaving the Suttons in a state of shock and bewilderment. As the first light of dawn painted the horizon, the family went outside to assess the damage. They found only bullet holes and a lingering sense of dread.

News of the Suttons' encounter with the strange beings quickly spread throughout the town, capturing the imagination of the locals. Skeptics and believers alike descended upon the farmhouse, hoping to uncover the truth behind the baffling events. The media caught wind of the story, and soon, the tale of the Hopkinsville goblins captured the nation's attention.

Over time, opinions regarding the veracity of the Suttons' story varied. Some dismissed the account as a hoax or as a result of extraterrestrial beings that paid a visit to that remote farmhouse. Regardless of the skeptics' doubts, the Sutton family remained steadfast in their conviction that the events of that night were all too real.

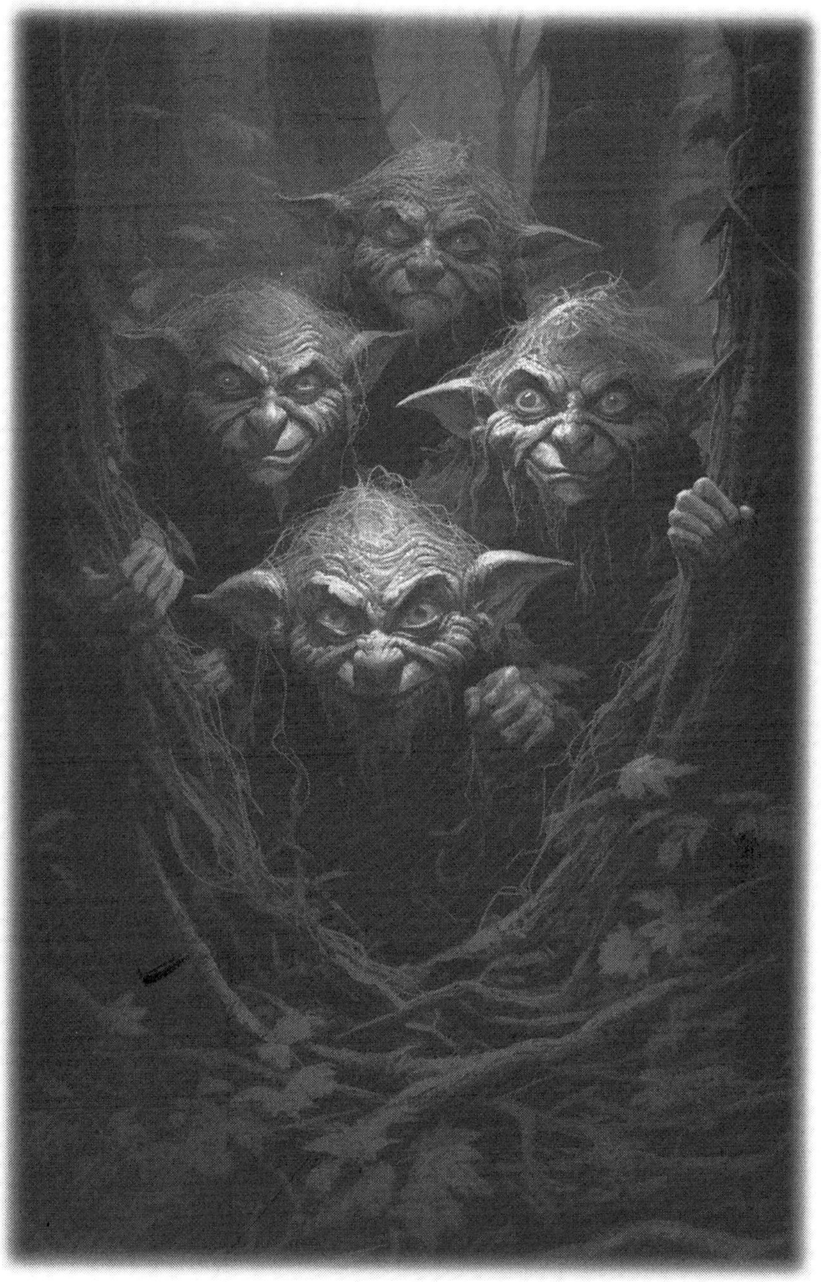

The White River Monster

For generations, the legend of the White River Monster had woven its way through the fabric of Arkansas folklore. In the heart of this tale was the White River, a major tributary of the Mississippi, where the mysterious creature has made its elusive presence known. In 1937, a surge of strange sightings ignited the flame of curiosity that would burn for decades to come.

Bramlett Bateman, a farmer that lived near the river, found himself at the center of this story. His affidavit, signed on July 1 of that year, detailed his extraordinary encounter with the creature. Bateman spoke of an unusual spectacle that lasted about five minutes. According to him, the creature was a serpent-like entity about 12 feet long and 4 or 5 feet wide. His testimony was only the beginning, for he claimed he knew of two dozen others who had similar accounts of the creature's existence.

The news of the sightings quickly spread, capturing the attention of large newspapers which made the White River Monster known all over the country. The creature became colloquially known as "Whitey," a nickname that stuck for generations and added to its mystique.

The folklore surrounding Whitey wasn't a new creation; its origins were traced back to the Quapaw Indians, who had stories of a serpent-like creature lurking in the river. The tale was handed down through time, gathering more layers of intrigue and mystery.

After Bramlett Bateman's affidavit, efforts were made to capture the creature, with plans for a massive rope net to snare the strange creature. However, the construction came to an abrupt halt due to financial constraints and lack of materials. Sightings began to dwindle and interest in the river monster faded away

Decades later, in 1971, sightings of Whitey reignited. Witness accounts varied, describing a creature with gray skin and spiny features, with some even claiming to see a horn protruding from its forehead. A trail of mysterious three-toed, fourteen-inch prints were found along the riverbanks, which baffled scientists and researchers. The sightings prompted state Senator Robert Harvey to pass a bill that established the White River Monster Refuge, an area where harming the creature was against the law.

As the years passed, the legend of Whitey continued to captivate the imagination of locals and visitors alike. Theories about the creature's identity ranged from a giant fish to an elephant seal. The White River Monster remains an enigma and has not been seen for a long time. Perhaps it will return again one day.

Midwest Monsters

The Okoboji Monster

In northwest Iowa you will find the East Okoboji Lake. This natural body of water in Dickinson County covers approximately 1,835 acres. Yet, beneath the surface, this lake conceals secrets and mysteries that have intrigued locals for generations.

East Okoboji Lake is often described as a paradox of depth, with an average depth of just 10 feet (3.0 meters) and a maximum depth of 22 feet. Its seemingly shallow waters belie the possibility of what may reside beneath.

The legend of East Okoboji Lake and its mysterious inhabitant dates back over a century. On July 3, 1903, an article was published in the Vindicator and Republican newspaper from Estherville, Iowa, recounting a chilling encounter experienced by Mr. and Mrs. Charles Bartlett.

The Bartletts were fishing that day, unaware that they were about to witness something they would never forget. As they rowed out onto the lake they saw something inexplicable. A commotion unfolded just a short distance from their boat. Whatever it was that caused the disturbance moved rapidly through the water, close to the surface, and appeared to be as massive as an overturned skiff.

The waves generated by this entity were so colossal that Mr. Bartlett found himself genuinely alarmed, fearing that his small boat might be capsized. However, he and his wife had no frame of reference for what they were witnessing. The Vindicator and Republican newspaper's account described it as such: "They saw something, or rather saw where something was. They have no idea what it was. It might have been a sea serpent, or it might have been some kind of fish that had grown to unusual and extraordinary size."

For many years following that eerie encounter in 1903, the waters of East Okoboji Lake remained remarkably quiet. No further sightings or reports of strange disturbances emerged to substantiate the Bartletts' claims.

However, the creature in the lake wouldn't be dormant forever. In 2001, a new chapter in the story of East Okoboji Lake Monster began to unfold when a local man noticed a large and peculiar creature in the water. This sighting marked the resurgence of interest in the lake's mysterious creature after uploading a video to YouTube. The video went viral and reignited curiosity about the secrets that East Okoboji Lake conceals.

East Okoboji Lake continues to lure the curious and the adventurous. The legend endures as the mystery of the lake's creature remains a compelling and enduring part of local lore.

The Devil's Lake Monster

In the heart of North Dakota, beneath the waters of Devil's Lake, an age-old legend has etched itself into the tapestry of local folklore—a colossal creature known as the Devil's Lake Monster. These tales, passed down through generations, find their roots in the stories shared by Native American tribes that inhabited these lands long before European settlers arrived.

Descriptions of this entity may vary, but a common thread weaves them together—a creature adorned with alligator-like jaws and piercing, fiery-red eyes that mirror the hues of a crimson sunset. As August's lazy days wane and the sun descends, the Devil's Lake Monster is said to emerge, casting eerie flashes of red light upon the water's surface. It's astonishing 80-foot tail leaves a shimmering wake as it glides through the depths of the lake. The serpent's movements are methodical and deliberate, tracing a circuit around the lake over the course of a day or two, maintaining a distance of about half a mile from the shore.

The creature's slimy green coloration, coupled with its sinuous form, creates distinctive waves of motion from head to tail. Formidable, ragged fins adorn its flanks, and the area around its jaws—indeed, just behind them—bears protrusions that trail along in the water. When provoked, these projections transform into a nightmarish, bristling display. The serpent's scales shift from a glistening sheen to lying flat against its back, resembling common snakeskin. Startled witnesses have recounted the serpent's sudden and tumultuous disruptions of the water, leaving foamy upheaval in its wake.

One such account back in 1915, involves a group of individuals taking a leisurely stroll along the Chautauqua grounds at Devil's Lake. Among them were Mrs. C.F. Craig of Leeds, Mrs. Edgar Larue, and Mrs. Carr Cleveland. Their walk along the lake's edge was abruptly interrupted when they spotted an object that resembled a sea serpent, approximately a mile from the shore. Retrieving opera glasses, they meticulously observed every detail. Their collective sighting sent shivers down their spines—the serpent, journeying northward across the lake, left behind an extensive wake, a testament to its immense size and power. Its thick, loathsome-looking black scales undulated through the water, while its serpent-like head boasted a darting tongue and eyes as large as goose eggs, glowing with an intense and unsettling fury.

Another sighting unfolded a short time later when a group of onlookers, including Emerson Lewis, a local businessman, observed a strange creature from a passing train near Devil's Lake. Though over a hundred years have gone by without a sighting, some claim that the monster is still lurking in the depths of Devil's Lake.

Mothman

In November 1966, a series of chilling events unfolded in the quiet town of Point Pleasant, West Virginia, setting the stage for the emergence of a cryptid known as the Mothman. It all began with gravediggers working in a cemetery in Clendenin, West Virginia, who spotted an eerie figure lurking in the trees above them, a foreshadowing of the inexplicable terror to come.

The unsettling saga of the Mothman began to take shape on November 15, 1966, when two young couples, Roger and Linda Scarberry, and Steve and Mary Mallette, reported an encounter with a bizarre and unsettling entity. The sighting took place near the old "TNT area," the site of a former World War II munitions plant. Linda Scarberry's description of the creature was nightmarish, a "slender, muscular man" standing approximately seven feet tall with wings that were stark white. However, her account was haunted by the creature's most sinister feature: its eyes, which glowed a malevolent red.

Distressed by this eerie encounter, the two couples fled in their car at breakneck speed. The creature relentlessly followed them until they reached the city limits of Point Pleasant.

The days that followed the initial encounter saw the emergence of more reports from other residents of Point Pleasant. Local newspapers spread the story, and additional sightings of the Mothman began to surface. Like the initial reports, the mysterious entity was said to be a winged creature with red, piercing eyes.

As the number of witnesses grew, speculation abounded about the origin and nature of this strange being. Some believed that the Mothman had taken up residence inside an abandoned power plant, which has since been demolished.

The sightings of the Mothman intensified over the following year, leaving the local community in a state of enduring dread. Some locals even began to speculate that the creature might be a product of a secret government experiment. Conspiracy theories ran rampant as the Mothman's reputation continued to grow.

However, the inexplicable and terrifying encounters ceased abruptly in December 1967, marked by a devastating tragedy that cast a shadow over Point Pleasant. On December 15, 1967, the Silver Bridge, a critical structure that spanned the Ohio River and connected Point Pleasant with Gallipolis, Ohio, suddenly collapsed under the weight of the heavy rush-hour traffic.

The cataclysmic event claimed the lives of 46 people, marking it as the deadliest bridge disaster in modern history.

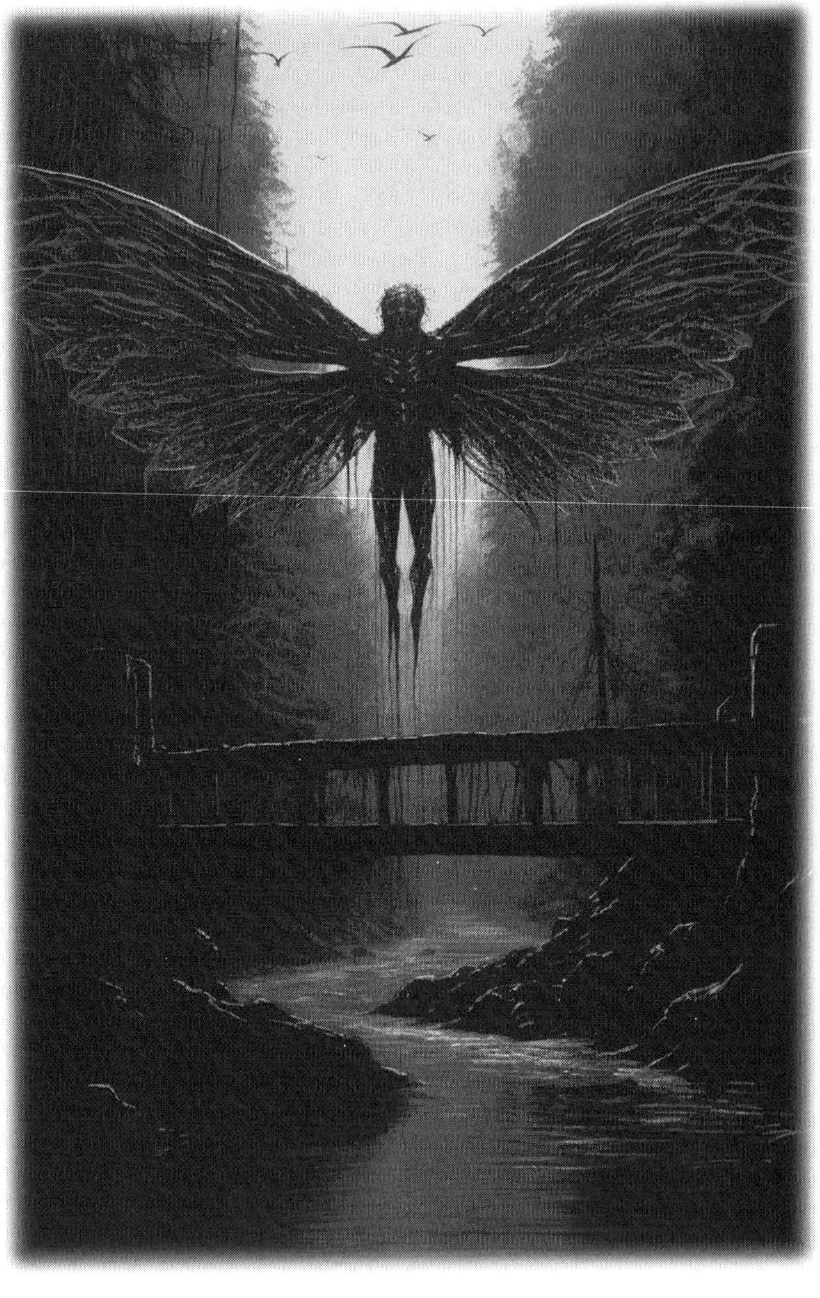

The Silver Bridge was a unique structure, the first of its kind in the United States, constructed using a revolutionary eyebar-link suspension system rather than traditional wire cables. However, a fatal flaw lay within this innovation—a single chain on each side supported the bridge decking, a lack of redundancy that proved catastrophic.

The failure of a single link in the chain, concealed by a stress fracture, led to the bridge's sudden collapse, sending 31 vehicles and their occupants plummeting into the frigid waters of the Ohio River.

In the wake of this tragic event, conspiracy theories began to circulate, speculating that the Mothman sightings were ominous warnings foretelling the bridge's collapse. In 1975, writer John Keel published "The Mothman Prophecies," connecting the Mothman phenomenon with the bridge disaster. This book popularized the eerie link between the cryptid and the tragic event, suggesting that the sightings served as harbingers of doom.

The tale of the Mothman and the Silver Bridge disaster captured the nation's imagination and inspired a 2002 film adaptation starring Richard Gere and Laura Linney.

Point Pleasant, the small town at the center of these events, fully embraced its most famous resident. The annual Mothman Festival began in 2002, a 12-foot metallic statue of the creature was erected in 2003, and the Mothman Museum and Research Center opened its doors in 2005.

Recently, however, the Mothman's has been seen in other parts of the country. Reports and sightings of this cryptid have surfaced in the Chicago, sending waves of unease through the Windy City. Whether this winged enigma is a harbinger of tragedy, or an entity still cloaked in mystery, the Mothman continues to haunt the realms of folklore.

Momo the Monster

In the town of Louisiana, Missouri, the summer of 1972 brought with it an unexpected visitor that would soon become the stuff of legend — Momo, the Missouri Monster. The phenomenon ignited after two young boys and their sister reported a spine-chilling sighting. They described a towering creature on the outskirts of the town.

One of the witnesses, Doris Harrison, a 15-year-old girl living at the base of Star Hill, vividly recounted her encounter with the creature. She claimed it was a monstrous entity, nearly 10 feet in height, standing on two legs like a man. Its body was covered in long, dark hair, and it held the carcass of a bleeding dog in one of its arms. The children swiftly informed their mother about the unnerving sighting. As she glanced outside, she heard a spine-chilling sound, starting as a low growl and rising to a whistle-like pitch. The children's father, upon returning home from work, led a search of the surroundings. Though they discovered traces of long black hair scattered across their property and noticed large footprints in the mud, they found no sign of the creature. Yet, the air was tainted with a putrid, moldy stench that lingered around their house.

Curiously, the sightings expanded as others in the neighborhood began encountering the bizarre figure. Several children even claimed to have spotted the tall creature while playing in the nearby woods.

The story of Momo's existence gained traction as additional sightings were reported. Richard Allan Murray, the local fire department chief and a city council member, shared his own unsettling experience. While driving along a creek bed, his headlights illuminated a colossal, upright figure cloaked in dark hair. Mere 20 feet away from him, the creature made a swift dash over a hill, disappearing from sight as it sensed Murray's presence.

As curiosity and fear swept through the town, a group of twenty people decided to form a posse to hunt down the elusive Momo. However, despite their efforts, the creature managed to remain elusive, leaving behind nothing but large footprints and a town forever marked by the eerie and unexplained.

The Wendigo

In the rich history of Plains and First Nations folklore, a chilling legend arises: the Wendigo. Once, it was a renowned hunter who roamed the wilderness, a legend among his people for his prowess and skill. But then, something changed, something dark and sinister that would cast a long shadow over his legacy.

The tale of the Wendigo begins with a lost hunter, driven to the brink by the merciless grip of a brutal winter. As the biting cold gnawed at his very soul, an insatiable hunger took root within him. The relentless craving for food led him down a path of darkness and desperation.

In a cruel twist of fate, the hunter turned to

the unthinkable, resorting to cannibalism as a means of survival. He partook in the forbidden feast of human flesh, an act that would forever seal his gruesome fate. With each bite, he devoured his own humanity, and in the depths of that frigid forest, he transformed into something beyond human comprehension.

The man became a monster, a nightmarish creature known as the Wendigo. Driven to madness by his heinous actions, the Wendigo became an insatiable predator, driven by an unquenchable thirst for more human flesh. He roamed the dense, snow-covered forests, lurking among the shadows, forever haunted by his insatiable hunger.

The legend of the Wendigo, sometimes spelled Windigo or Windego, originates from the folklore of Algonquian Native American tribes. While the specifics of the tale may vary among different cultures, there is a common thread that binds them together. Some have likened the Wendigo to a relative of Bigfoot, while others draw parallels with the lore of the werewolf.

The Wendigo's haunting presence is often associated with cold-weather regions, predominantly in Canada and the northern states of the United States, such as Minnesota.

In the early 20th century, Algonquian tribes attributed many unsolved disappearances to the nefarious deeds of the Wendigo. This strange creature, despite its emaciated appearance, stands nearly 15 feet tall, a towering monstrosity always driven by its insatiable appetite for human flesh.

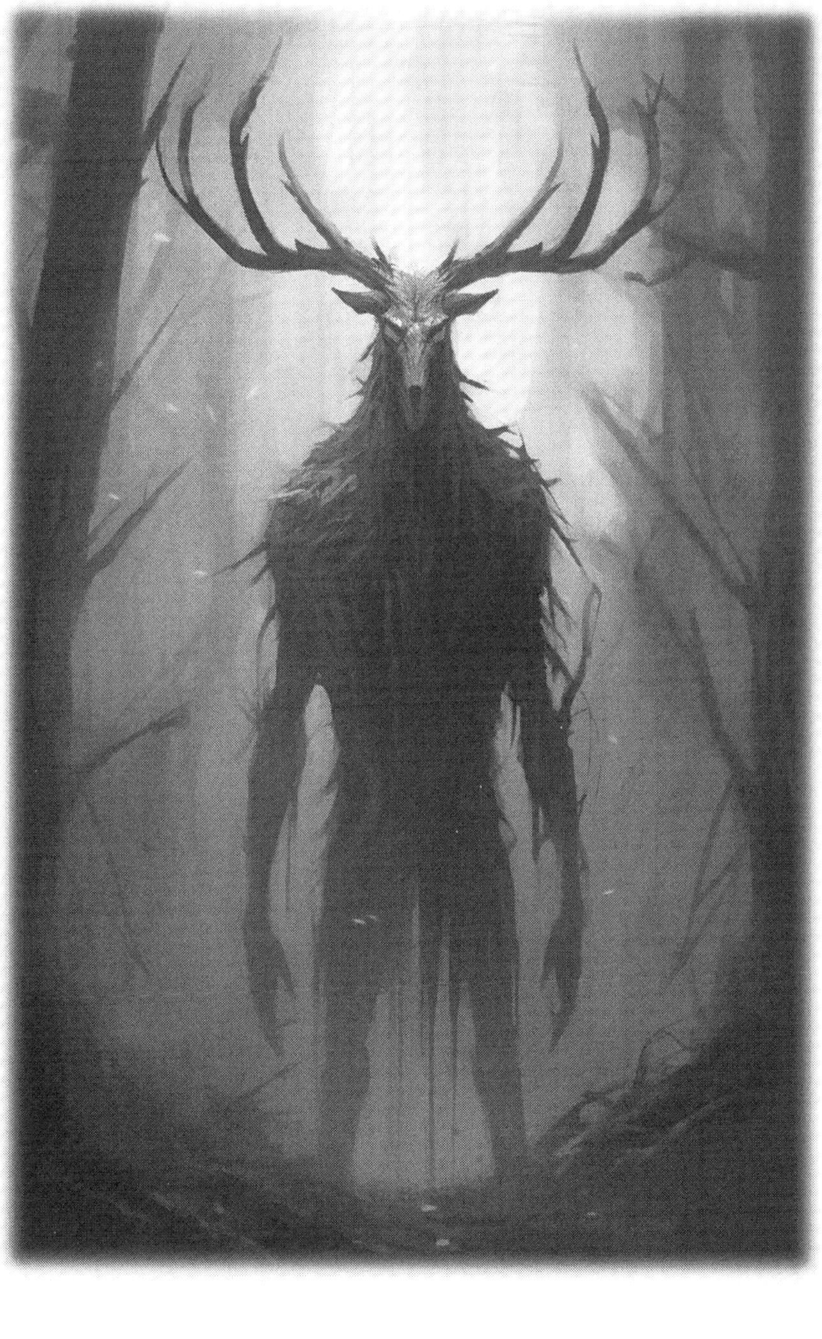

The Wendigo, with its voracious hunger, poses an unsettling question: are these creatures mere figments of Native American mythology, or do they lurk in the shadows of our forests, waiting for their next unfortunate victim?

The legends of the Wendigo are not limited to the Algonquian people alone; various Native American tribes, including the neighboring Iroquois, share tales of similar entities. The term "Wendigo," roughly translated, signifies "the evil spirit that devours mankind." Another interpretation, dating back to a German explorer's account from around 1860, equates the term with "cannibal."

These malevolent beings are deeply associated with cold, winter, and famine. The Algonquian legend paints a vivid image of the Wendigo: "a giant with a heart of ice, sometimes thought to be entirely made of ice, with a skeletal and deformed body, lacking lips and toes." The Ojibwa's account describes it as "a large creature, as tall as a tree, with a lipless mouth and jagged teeth. Its breath makes a hissing sound, its footprints drip with blood, and it feasts upon any unfortunate soul who ventures into its territory. Those possessed by the Wendigo themselves hunt down their friends and families and feast on their flesh."

The Wendigo is as much a hunter as it is a cannibal, employing stealth and supernatural skills. It is a master of its territory, controlling the weather through dark magic and perpetually hunting for its next meal. Paradoxically, despite its gluttony, the Wendigo is emaciated, tormented by an insatiable hunger for human flesh.

While the legend of the Wendigo is deeply rooted in Native American folklore, it has also found its way into popular culture. In 2023, Party City even immortalized the Wendigo by creating a Halloween animatronic based on this terrifying creature, ensuring that its eerie legend endures in the modern world.

Southwest Legends

The Chupacabra

The eerie legend of the Chupacabra, whose name translates to "goat sucker" in Spanish, has cast its shadow over Latin American folklore for many years. While the first recorded sightings of this cryptid date back to the mid-1970s, it wasn't until the 1990s that the Chupacabra began to garner widespread attention, and it continues to be a source of intrigue and fear, particularly in the southwestern regions of the United States, such as Texas.

The Chupacabra was first associated with a series of perplexing events in the Rio Grande Valley of South Texas during the mid-1970s. Reports emerged of what some believed to be a condor, a massive bird, which was linked to a rash of mutilated cattle. These unfortunate animals were found with every drop of their blood mysteriously drained, a gruesome and eerie sight that baffled ranchers and investigators alike.

The early 1970s witnessed another unsettling encounter in Brownsville, Texas. A rancher stumbled upon a lifeless bull, its blood also drained, and perplexingly, no tracks or traces to offer a clue as to what had transpired.

However, it wasn't until May 2, 1996, that the Chupacabra's reputation truly took hold in the Rio Grande Valley of South Texas. On that day, a pet goat was discovered lifeless, its neck marked by three puncture wounds. The wounds were reminiscent of the so-called "telltale marks" of the Chupacabra, setting off a wave of speculation and dread among the locals.

By this point, the legend of the Chupacabra had now taken a firm foothold in the United States, particularly in the arid landscapes of Texas. Reports of strange creatures prowling the countryside, striking terror into the hearts of farmers and ranchers, became increasingly common.

While these early accounts gave rise to fear and fascination, they were merely the prelude to a series of more recent sightings and encounters that have continued to perplex and amaze residents of the Lone Star State.

Over the years, various sightings have added to the creature's mystique. These included encounters in Cuero in 2007, a 2014 case where a Texas family claimed to have captured a Chupacabra in a cage, and a 2016 sighting in Hockley County, West Texas. In 2019, a photograph that appeared to depict the Chupacabra was taken on Highway 6 in Houston.

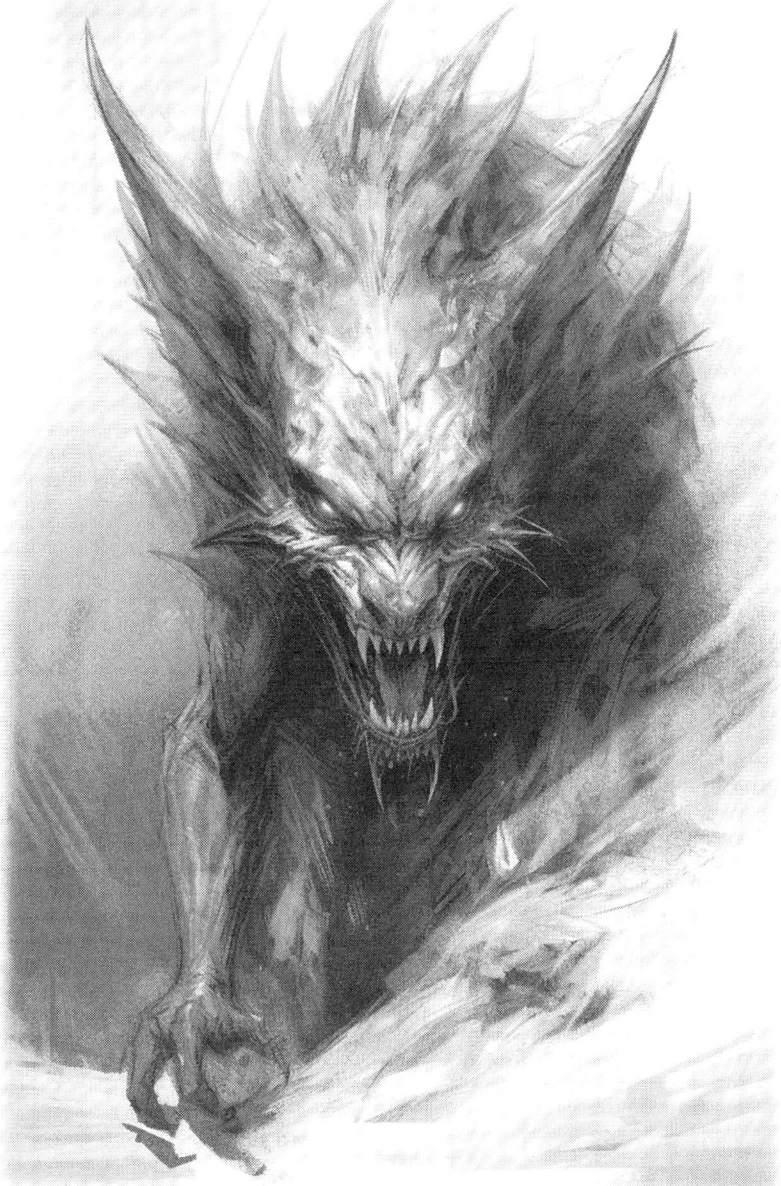

However, one of the most intriguing sightings occurred in 2022. Surveillance footage captured a bipedal, wolf-like creature lurking outside the Amarillo Zoo during the summer months. This chilling incident raised questions about the nature of the Chupacabra and whether it was a mere legend or a real creature.

Despite skepticism and alternative explanations, the Chupacabra remains a captivating part of Texas folklore. It continues to make appearances in sensational documentaries and local news reports, keeping the mystery alive and well in the hearts of those who inhabit rural communities in central Texas and beyond.

As the legend of the Chupacabra has evolved over the years, skeptics have posited various theories to explain these sightings. Some suggest that the creature may have been a person in a costume, while others propose more mundane explanations, such as a coyote, a dog, or a large raccoon afflicted with mange.

Nonetheless, the Chupacabra endures as one of the most enduring and popular cryptids in Texas.

The Bear King

In Southeast Texas, in Marble Falls, a tribe of Kickapoo Indians held a local legend that caused generations of young men and women to live in fear- the legend of the "Bear King," a creature that reigned supreme over all the bears in that wilderness.

In 1901 there was a young and lovely girl named Ramie Arland, known to be the prettiest maiden in the area. One day after the sun went down, Ramie was tending to her family's sheep. The tranquil landscape was disrupted when her mother, inside their home, suddenly heard a series of blood-curdling screams. Fearing the worst, she dashed outside, clutching her rifle, convinced that a panther had attacked her daughter.

Frantic and trembling with dread, Mrs. Arland ventured into the woods that surrounded their home, but despite her search, there was no sign of her Ramie.

Determined to find her daughter, she hurried back home, gathering the neighbors for an impromptu hunting party to scour the woods. But despite their combined efforts, Ramie had vanished into thin air.

It was only on the dawn of the following day that a twist of fate led to a startling discovery. A hunter, deep within the wilderness, stumbled upon Ramie Arland, disheveled and wandering aimlessly in a field on the outskirts of their small town.

The hunter, bewildered by the unexpected encounter, extended his hand to help her. Ramie Arland, in a voice trembling with fear and bewilderment, began to recount the spine-chilling events that had unfolded during her disappearance.

Ramie had been strolling along a narrow trail near her family's home when, without warning, a colossal bear emerged from the shadows. Her heart pounded as she gazed upon this imposing creature, but her terror multiplied when an even larger, more fearsome bear joined the scene, causing the first bear to slink away into the shadows. This towering, commanding presence, Ramie believed, was none other than the infamous Bear King of Indian legend.

The Bear King approached the young girl, its massive form casting a daunting shadow. Its fierce, dark eyes locking onto hers as it emitted an eerie and unearthly roar that sent tremors through her very soul. She believed her life to be hanging by a thread, expecting the bear to strike her down. Yet, to her astonishment, the creature didn't attack. Instead, it gently took hold of her and began to transport her toward the foreboding mountains that loomed in the distance.

After what felt like an eternity, the bear reached a desolate cave, where it carefully laid her upon some rocks. In a moment of sheer desperation, Ramie seized an opportunity when she believed the creature wasn't watching and fled. But her escape was thwarted when the Bear King struck her with its massive paw, sending her sprawling to the ground.

Time seemed to stretch on indefinitely, and at last, the Bear King finally began to get tired. When Ramie was convinced that the creature was soundly asleep, she mustered every ounce of courage she possessed and took off running once more, fleeing from the monster's ominous lair.

Her description of the Bear King was nothing short of extraordinary; she called it a "bear man," an entity that ran on all fours, a grotesque hybrid of beast and human.

News of Ramie's ordeal spread like wildfire, stirring a mix of emotions among the townspeople—fear, disbelief, and curiosity. Armed with an assortment of weapons and an unwavering resolve, a group of men set out on a perilous expedition to track down the Bear King and investigate the cave that Ramie Arland had identified as its den.

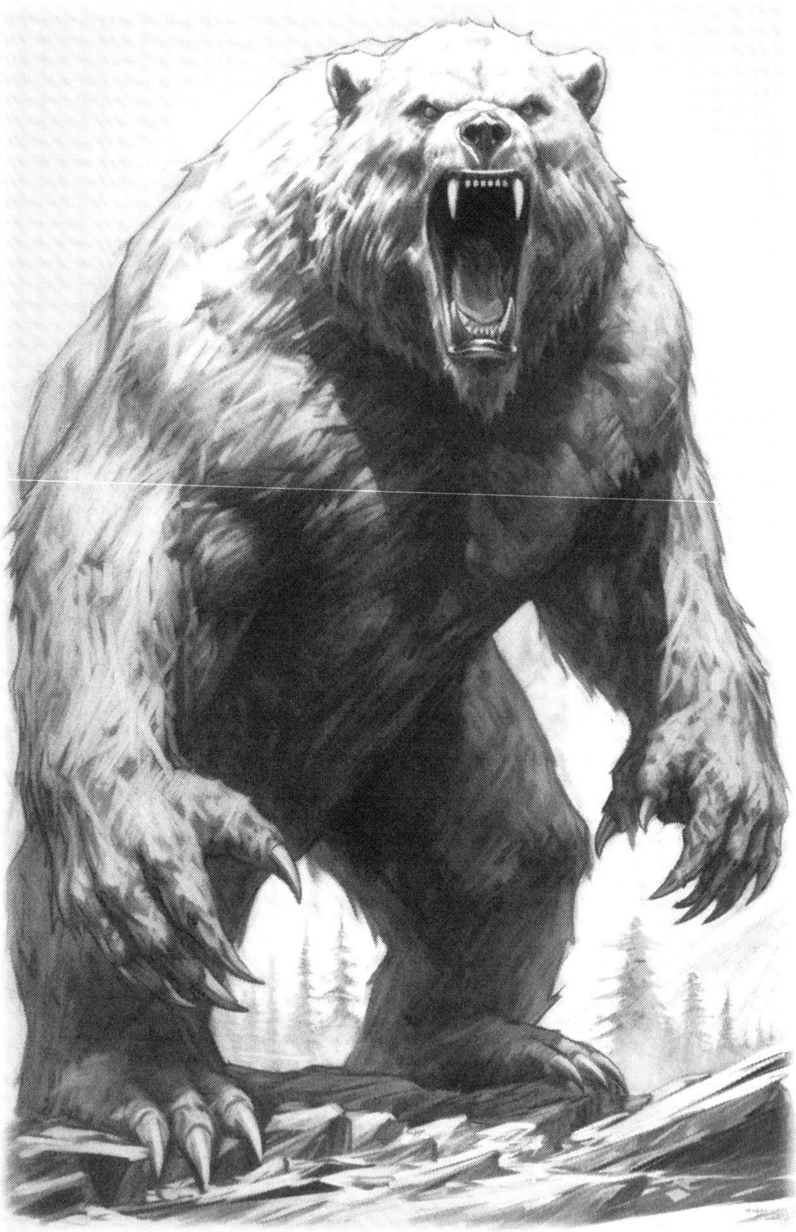

When they reached the cave, the Bear King was waiting, a looming and menacing presence. It began to growl, mimicking the chilling sounds of a panther, and pounded its chest in a display of fierce dominance. The men, torn between their own humanity and the grim reality before them, hesitated to take a life of a bear that somewhat resembled a human. But the creature left them with no choice; it charged at them with terrifying ferocity. Reluctantly, the men opened fire, ending the Bear King's reign of terror once and for all.

The legend of the Bear King, born from the whispers of the Kickapoo Indians and etched into the annals of Marble Falls history, had met its tragic and violent end.

The Lake Worth Monster

In the town of Lakeside, Texas nestled on the shores of Lake Worth in Texas, a creature of myth and terror once cast a shadow of fear over the community. This creature, known as the Lake Worth Monster, became the subject of local legend and national intrigue, leaving an indelible mark on the town's history.

In 1969 residents of Lake Worth began to report sightings of a bizarre and fearsome creature roaming the area. Descriptions of the creature varied, but a common thread among all accounts was its terrifying appearance and its eerie ability to blend into the surrounding landscape.

Witnesses claimed that the Lake Worth Monster resembled a cross between a human and a goat, standing approximately seven feet tall and covered in matted, fur-covered scales. Its hands ended in long, sharp claws, and its legs were powerful and muscular. But perhaps the most striking and unsettling feature of the creature were its piercing, glowing red eyes that seemed to radiate malevolence.

The monster's reign of terror began with a series of strange incidents. Reports included the creature hurling large rocks at cars and people. It also tossed a tire from an overpass onto the road below. These acts of aggression fueled rumors and spread fear throughout the community.

One of the most well-known encounters occurred on July 10, 1969, when a group of teens claimed to have spotted the Lake Worth Monster perched on the roof of a car. The creature reportedly leaped down onto the vehicle, leaving behind scratches and a lasting impression of terror on the witnesses.

As word spread and media attention grew, a group of locals set out to capture the creature and put an end to the reign of fear. Armed with rifles and a determination to uncover the truth, they embarked on a hunt that would ultimately lead to a controversial and debated encounter.

On July 11, a man named Allen Plaster claimed to have seen the creature and shot it with a tranquilizer dart. The monster supposedly let out a blood-curdling scream before plummeting into the waters of Lake Worth and disappearing beneath the surface. Despite efforts to retrieve the creature's body, it was never recovered.

In the aftermath, skeptics dismissed the Lake Worth Monster as a hoax or the result of overactive imaginations. Others clung to the belief that the creature was real, perhaps a wayward cryptid or an unknown species that had somehow found its way to the town.

Regardless of the true nature of the Lake Worth Monster, its legacy endures in the town's folklore.

The Oklahoma Octopus

In the heartland of Oklahoma, within the waters of Lake Thunderbird, Lake Tenkiller, and Lake Oolagah, lies a chilling mystery that has both perplexed and terrified the local communities. These manmade lakes, built in the mid-20th century have birthed a legend of unimaginable proportions – the Oklahoma Octopus.

The origin of this eerie legend can be traced back over two centuries, to the time when Native Americans spoke of an aquatic monster with a sinister appetite for human flesh. These tales, passed down through generations, have echoed through time, casting a shadow of dread over the waters of Oklahoma's lakes.

The creature, said to be as large as a horse or a small vehicle, possesses a strikingly reddish-brown hue, its skin resembling weathered leather. Its most chilling feature, however, is its long, sinuous tentacles or arms that extend menacingly into the murky depths. These nightmarish appendages are thought to be the instrument of its predatory instincts, waiting to ensnare unsuspecting swimmers.

The Oklahoma Octopus has been associated with a series of unexplained and tragic incidents that have unfolded on the lakes. Stories of drownings, accidents, and individuals who have vanished without a trace have fostered fear and uncertainty among the community. Over the years, these tales have multiplied, and a growing number of people have become convinced that something malevolent lurks beneath the surface, hunting those who dare to venture too far from the safety of the shore.

In 2013, a harrowing incident unfolded at Lake Thunderbird, cementing the Oklahoma Octopus's ominous reputation. A 59-year-old man was unloading his boat at the Little Axe Recreation Area. As his boat began to drift off into the lake, he made the fateful decision to swim out and retrieve it. Tragically, he went under the water and remained unseen for several hours until his remains were finally recovered, leaving a community in shock.

A year later, another tragedy struck Lake Thunderbird. A man known to be a good swimmer, decided to swim across the lake. As he ventured a hundred yards from the shore, he suddenly disappeared beneath the surface. Later that night, his lifeless body was discovered, further fueling the unsettling tales of the Oklahoma Octopus.

2021 brought yet another chilling incident, this time involving a man who was swimming with a float in Lake Thunderbird. In a sudden and inexplicable turn of events, he too vanished beneath the surface. As evening fell, his remains were found, adding another chapter to the dark legend of the Oklahoma Octopus.

The idea of a freshwater-dwelling octopus might appear far-fetched, as these creatures are primarily known to inhabit saltwater. Adapting to entirely freshwater conditions would require extraordinary physiological transformations, which no cephalopod has been known to achieve. Furthermore, the timeline of Oklahoma's lakes, mostly engineered in the 20th century, presents a logistical challenge for any creature to navigate its way upstream, past multiple dams.

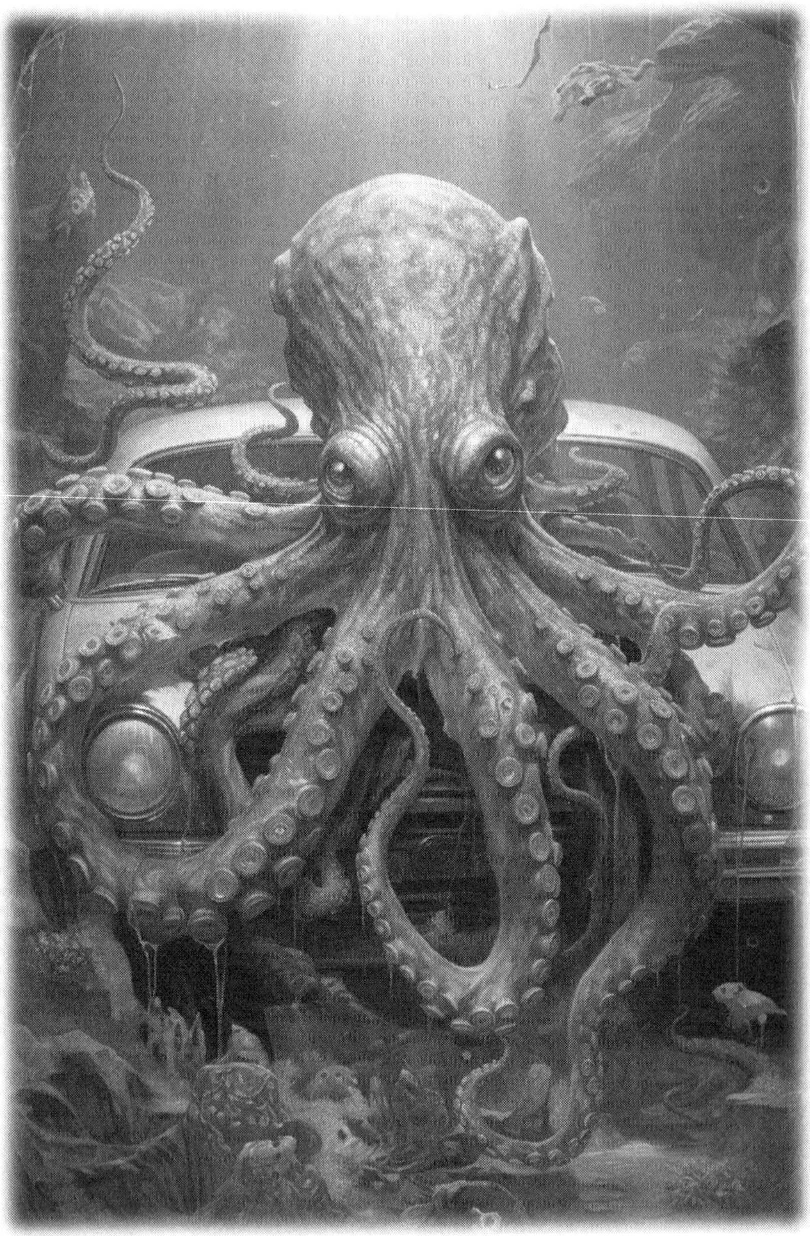

Unlike other cryptids, the legend of the Oklahoma Octopus refuses to wane with time. Instead, it continues to grow, its sinister reputation preceding it. As the mystery deepens and the unexplained tragedies persist, a shroud of dread hangs over these lakes.

The Mogollon Monster

In the remote wilderness of Arizona's Mogollon Rim, a shadowy legend has endured for generations - the Mogollon Monster, a creature steeped in mystery and fear. This elusive cryptid, believed to inhabit the dense forests and rugged canyons of the region, has captivated the imagination of locals and adventurous souls alike.

The tale of the Mogollon Monster dates back to the indigenous peoples who have lived in the area for centuries. Their legends spoke of a towering, ape-like creature that roamed the woods, rarely seen but occasionally leaving behind colossal footprints and ominous howls that chilled the night air.

As time passed, settlers and ranchers in the Mogollon Rim region also began to share their own eerie encounters. They described a massive, hulking beast covered in matted fur, with fiery red eyes that gleamed in the moonlight. Stories of livestock and pets disappearing, along with eerie nocturnal screams fueled the legend further.

One of the most famous encounters with the Mogollon Monster occurred in the 1940s when a group of prospectors claimed to have stumbled upon the creature while deep in the wilderness. They reported that it stood over seven feet tall, with a stench that reeked of sulfur and decay. Terrified, the prospectors fled, leaving behind their campsite and their gold.

In the decades that followed, sightings and encounters with the Mogollon Monster became a part of local lore. Some speculated that it was a reclusive Bigfoot or a cousin of the elusive Sasquatch, while others believed it to be a cryptid unique to the Mogollon Rim.

Despite numerous expeditions and investigations by cryptozoologists and paranormal enthusiasts, concrete evidence of the creature's existence remained elusive. Grainy photographs, unidentifiable footprints, and eerie vocal recordings can easily be dismissed.

Whether the Mogollon Monster is a product of folklore, misidentification, or an actual unknown species hidden in the depths of Arizona's wilderness, its legend continues to cast a long and eerie shadow over the rugged landscapes of the Mogollon Rim.

Cryptids of the West

The Dark Watchers

Deep within the untamed beauty of California's Santa Lucia Mountains, an age-old mystery endures—the Dark Watchers. These shadowy figures, known for their silent vigil, continue to captivate our imagination, leaving an indelible mark on the region's folklore.

Renowned author John Steinbeck, in his masterpiece "Flight," alluded to these elusive figures, bringing the legend of the Dark Watchers to a wider audience.

"Pepé looked suspiciously back every minute or so, and his eyes sought the tops of the ridges ahead," Steinbeck wrote. "Once, on a white barren spur, he saw a black figure for a moment; but he looked quickly away, for it was one of the dark watchers. No one knew who the watchers were, nor where they lived, but it was better to ignore them and never to show interest in them. They did not bother one who stayed on the trail and minded his own business."

His words cast a literary spotlight on these spectral beings, connecting them to the fabric of California's rich storytelling tradition.

The folklore of the Dark Watchers dates back centuries among indigenous peoples like the Chumash. These shadowy beings, often described as tall and cloaked, are said to silently observe travelers in the mountains. The legends speak of them as both protectors and omens, appearing during twilight and dawn, only to vanish when approached.

Despite countless sightings and anecdotes, the true nature of the Dark Watchers remains elusive. Are they supernatural guardians, ancient spirits, or simply a trick of the light? Scholars, scientists, and seekers of the paranormal have all sought to uncover the truth behind this enduring legend.

The Dark Watchers' affinity for twilight hours adds to their mystique. Some speculate that the phenomenon may be a result of atmospheric conditions. Others maintain that these entities are interdimensional beings, drawn to the liminal space between night and day.

Steinbeck's literary legacy lives on, as does the age-old legend of the Dark Watchers.

The Billiwhack Monster

In the heart of Ventura County, California a mysterious tale took root in the 1940s, revolving around the site of the former Billiwhack Dairy. This story was laced with rumors, secrets, and the ominous figure known as the Billiwhack Monster.

August Rubel, a German national, was the owner of the dairy during World War II. Whispers in the community hinted at a secret underground lab beneath the dairy, where Rubel was allegedly collaborating with the U.S. government on the development of a super soldier for wartime purposes. It was a precarious endeavor, and in 1943, Rubel embarked on a treacherous journey back to his native Germany, supposedly working as a covert operative for the Allies. Tragically, he met his end on that journey when he stepped on a German landmine.

Years later, the abandoned grounds of the Billiwhack Dairy became the breeding ground for unsettling reports. Local high school students began recounting eerie encounters with a bizarre creature, described as a towering humanoid with goat-like horns and razor-sharp claws. This creature wasn't content merely with lurking; it had a penchant for hurling hefty rocks at passing cars, striking fear into the hearts of those in the area who crossed its path.

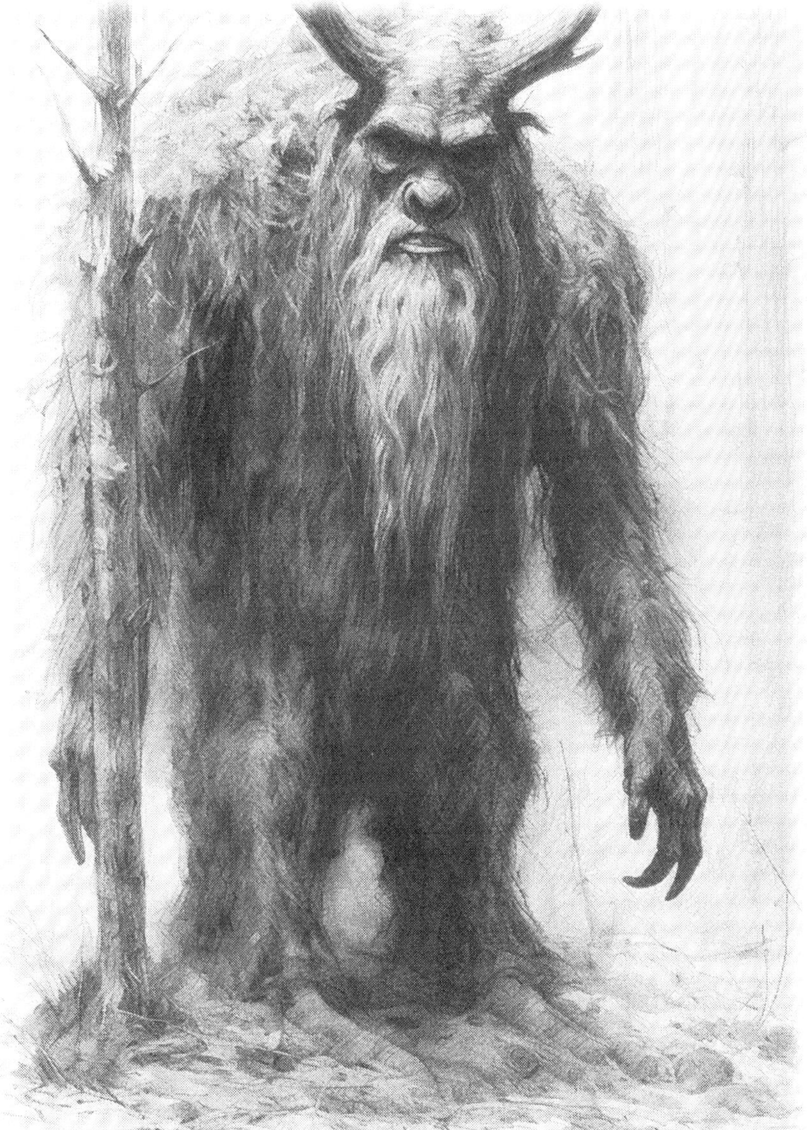

The legend of the Billiwhack Monster persisted, and in 1964, some hikers claimed to see a hairy monstrosity adorned with ram's horns, which stalked them relentlessly for hours through the wilderness. Some locals found themselves victimized, as their vehicles became targets for the creature's violent pounding.

This creature, known as the Billiwhack Monster, embodied the nightmares of local residents. Standing tall, muscular, and covered in gray hair, it was the stuff of legends. Some versions of the tale even portrayed it as a spectral being, haunting the land it once roamed.

In the 1950s, a nine-year-old claimed to have been attacked by the mysterious menace, bearing ghastly wounds inflicted by its clawed hands. The 1960s witnessed a surge in reports, with accounts of the monster wielding a massive club or launching large rocks at unsuspecting passersby.

The Billiwhack Monster's legacy became an enduring enigma in Ventura County, a tale that blurred the line between reality and the supernatural, and a chilling reminder of the mysteries that can hide within the most unexpected places.

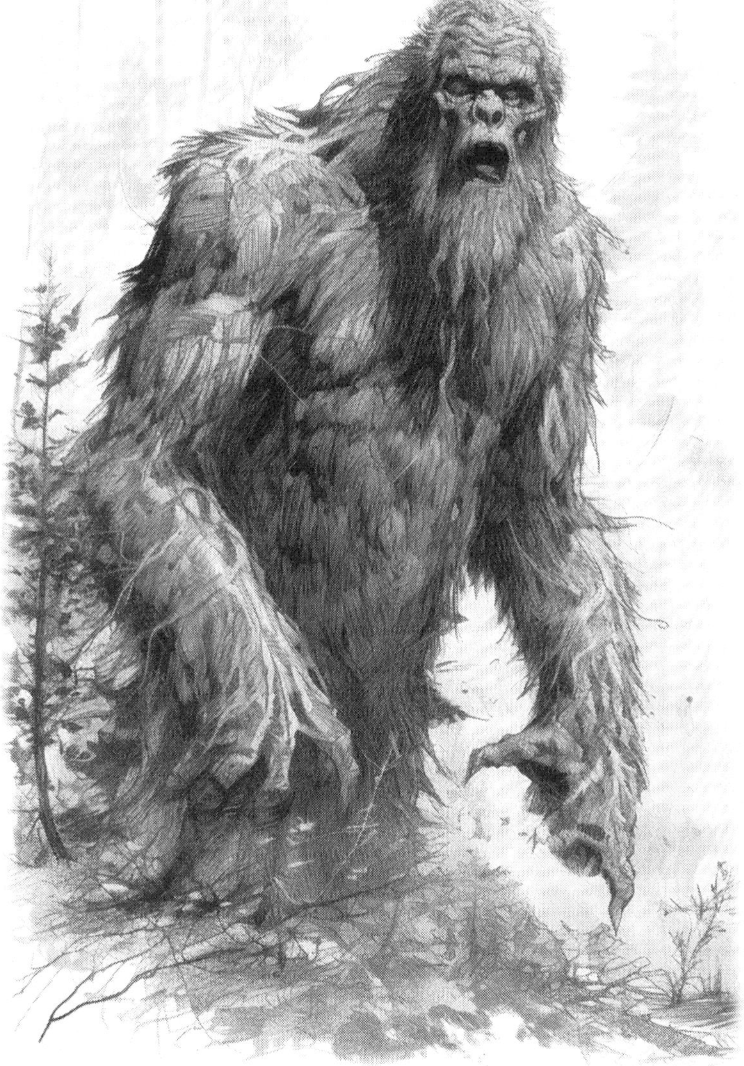

The Fresno Nightcrawler

In the quiet hours of a chilly Fresno night, an eerie presence stirred in the shadows. Little did anyone know that they were about to bear witness to an otherworldly phenomenon — the Fresno Nightcrawler.

The story reached a fever pitch in 2014 when surveillance cameras around Fresno, California, began capturing inexplicable footage. The mysterious beings were tall, slender, and pale, resembling ethereal specters with no discernible facial features. These figures appeared to glide gracefully through the night, their elongated legs swaying like willow branches in the breeze.

However, the first documented sighting occurred in the yard of a local resident a few year earlier. His security camera captured the surreal image of a Fresno Nightcrawler passing through his property, seemingly uninterested in the human world.

As news of these bizarre creatures spread, more people came forward with their own recordings. Witnesses reported that the Nightcrawlers moved with an almost hypnotic grace, as if they were dancing through the darkness. Their existence became a topic of debate among paranormal enthusiasts, skeptics, and scientists alike.

Some speculated that the Nightcrawlers were extraterrestrial beings, while others believed them to be supernatural entities from another dimension. Skeptics offered more grounded explanations, suggesting that these peculiar figures were merely the result of video manipulation or a clever hoax.

Yet, no one could deny the unsettling feeling that the Nightcrawlers evoked. Those who had seen them on camera or, in rare cases, with their own eyes, spoke of an eerie sensation that accompanied their appearance—a sense of being watched by something beyond comprehension.

Despite numerous investigations, the mystery of the Fresno Nightcrawler remains unsolved.

The Elizabeth Lake Monster

Nestled in the arid wilderness of Los Angeles County lies Elizabeth Lake, a place where legends intertwine with the land. The story begins with the ominous name "Laguna del Diablo" or "Devil's Lagoon," a nod to the belief that the Devil himself created the lake, keeping one of his otherworldly pets within its depths.

Early settlers bore witness to eerie occurrences. In the 1830s, Don Pedro Carrillo abandoned his lakeside ranch after several structures mysteriously burned to the ground in a single night. Reports of strange nocturnal noises and unnatural sightings plagued subsequent settlers, leading them to flee in fear.

Then, the creature itself made its presence known. Described as over 50 feet long with bat wings, a bulldog's head, wide neck, long legs, and an overpowering stench, it left an indelible mark on those who claimed to encounter it. The very ground beneath the lake, resting atop the San Andreas fault line, seemed to amplify the aura of the unknown.

The tales of Elizabeth Lake's monster are woven with intrigue and mystique, where reality and folklore blur. From the Spanish settlers' eerie experiences to the unexplained vanishing of livestock, the lake has kept its secrets well-guarded.

Miguel Leonis, the last to report an encounter with the creature, claimed to have injured it during an attack, prompting it to fly away. The legend lives on in Arizona, where a creature resembling Elizabeth Lake's monster is said to have been found dead.

Was it a true creature of the desert, a misidentification, or perhaps something supernatural? Regardless, the legend of Elizabeth Lake's monster still endures.

Tahoe Tessie

Located in the Sierra Nevada mountains, Lake Tahoe boasts the distinction of being the largest freshwater lake in the state of California. This pristine, crystal-clear body of water has long held a place in local lore as a repository of secrets, both ancient and mysterious.

Among these tales, two distinct myths have captured the imagination of those who call this region home.

The first of these myths alludes to a chilling tale of an underwater mob graveyard, a sinister burial ground that has remained shrouded in secrecy. According to local legend, the lake's 900-foot-deep waters, specifically off the South Shore, served as a covert dumping ground for the remains of gangsters from the 1920s to the 1950s. The frigid depths of the lake were believed to preserve the corpses and prevent their gruesome remains surfacing in a gas-bloated state, thus preventing exposure of their dark deeds. So pervasive was this belief that many local fishermen came to refer to the area as "The Graveyard."

Another myth harkens to the deep, unknown creatures lurking beneath the lake's surface. It speaks of a serpent-like being known as "Tessie," an apparent counterpart to the famous "Nessie" of Loch Ness. While Washoe Indian legend hints at Tessie's existence, it was in the 19th century that the creature first drew the attention of settlers in the area.

The year 1984 marked a significant turning point in the legend of Tessie when the San Francisco Chronicle reported an encounter with the Lake Tahoe monster. Two women, Patsy McKay and Diane Stavarakas, claimed to have seen the creature while hiking along the west shore. According to McKay, Tessie was an astonishing 17 feet long, repeatedly surfacing "like a little submarine." Stavarakas concurred, describing a beast with a humped back that emerged in a whale-like, lethargic manner.

Two years prior, off-duty policemen Kris Beebe and Jerry Jones encountered a similar creature. While water-skiing on the lake in June 1982, they encountered an "unusually large" creature swimming near them. Despite the initial shock of the sighting, Beebe recalled, "We saw it. It wasn't threatening us. It was just gliding past us. Was I scared? I believe I went into a state of shock!"

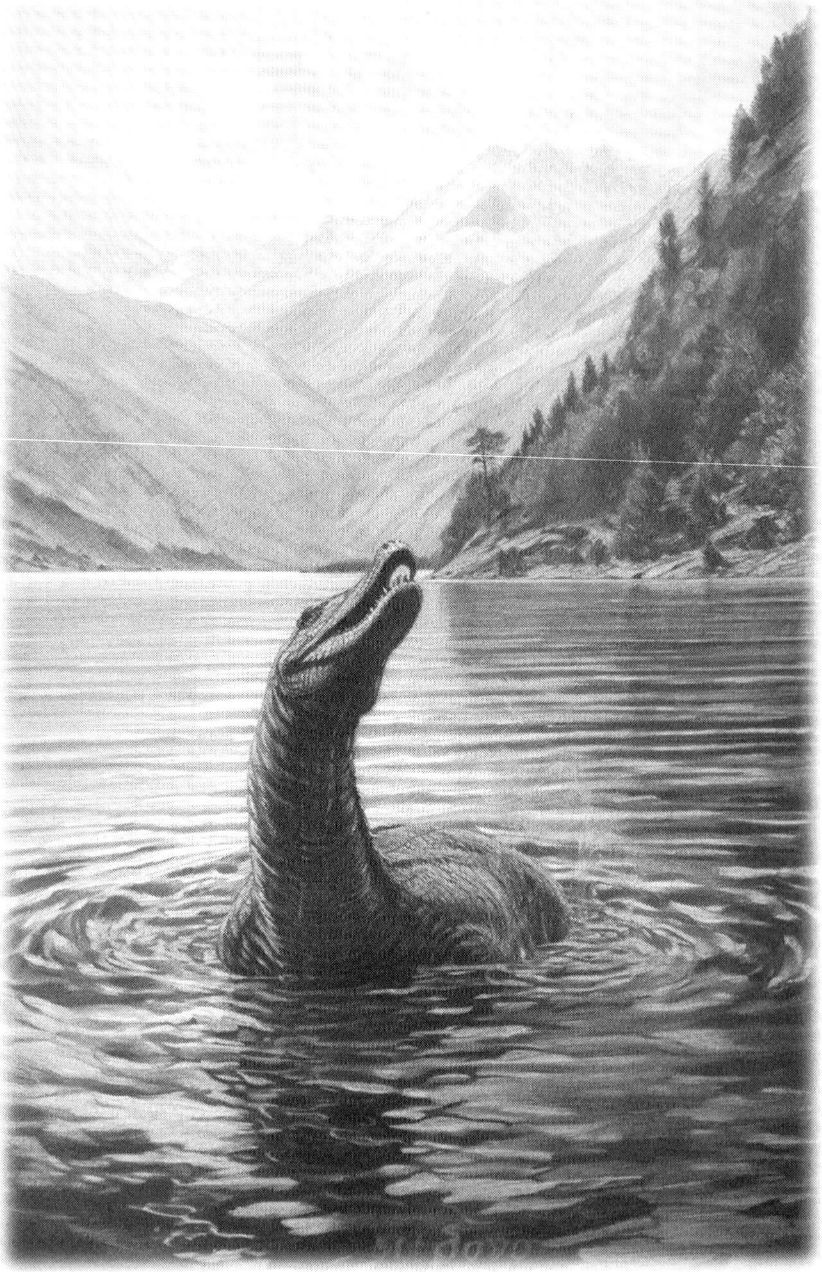

The descriptions of Tessie vary but some claim to see a large 30-foot-long creature like the Loch Ness Monster with a lizard-like head and long neck. Others have seen a black serpent-like entity or a green reptile.

However, some speculate that the mysterious creature could be a giant sturgeon, capable of growing to 12 feet long. Nevertheless, no sturgeon has ever been captured in Lake Tahoe.

Lake Tahoe's depth, reaching an astonishing 1,645 feet, provides ample room for Tessie to elude people. It could live in an underwater lair beneath the Cave Rock on the East Shore.

While the tales of Tessie and the mob graveyard in Lake Tahoe remain entwined in mystery and speculation, they continue to captivate the imagination of those who seek to uncover the secrets hidden beneath the lake's shimmering surface.

Northwest Lore

The Legend of Colossal Claude

In March 1934, aboard the Columbia River Lightship, the crew's daily routine took a surreal turn when they witnessed a creature like no other. L.A. Larson, first mate, and the entire crew encountered the monstrous Colossal Claude, a sea serpent that emerged from the depths of the Columbia River in Wenatchee, Oregon. With a body roughly 40 feet long, an 8-foot neck, and a menacingly sinuous tail, Claude's eerie form etched itself into their memories.

Claude's snaky head, resembling a blend of evil and menace, incited a mix of fascination and fear among the crew. Opinions varied regarding the creature's appearance; some described its head as resembling a camel, while others noted its snake-like characteristics.

The crew wanted to approach the colossal serpent in a small boat but were cautioned to stay away by officers who deemed it too risky. With a potential to capsize a boat, the massive creature maintained an air of danger. Eventually, Colossal Claude melted into the waters and disappeared.

Years later, the myth resurfaced with the crew of the trawler Viv and J. W. White and his wife, who each spotted the beast in separate instances. Descriptions varied from a "long, hairy, tan-colored creature" to an "aquatic giraffe," each sighting contributing to the creature's enigma.

However, the most infamous encounter came in 1939 when the crew of the Argo reported passing within arm's reach of the monster. Captain Chris Anderson watched in amazement as the creature's head and neck loomed 10 feet above the waves, a surreal spectacle that seemed almost otherworldly.

As time moved on, the legend of Colossal Claude held its place in maritime lore. Despite varying descriptions and skeptics, the essence of the creature's presence, its uncanny features, and its eerie allure persisted. The waters of the Columbia River continue to carry its secrets.

The Bear Lake Monster

In the heart of the serene Bear Lake Valley, where the borders of Utah and Idaho converge, a deep and mysterious lake holds a secret. It is a secret whispered through generations; a legend known to all – the Bear Lake Monster.

The origins of this extraordinary creature could be traced back to the sacred tales of Native American folklore, where it was known as 'Old Ephraim.' This creature, so the legends went, was not a mere figment of imagination but a serpent-like being, crowned with small horns upon its head.

The indigenous spoke of a beast with a haunting roar that echoed across the lake's calm surface.

Despite the skepticism and the relentless attempts to either capture or debunk the existence of the Bear Lake Monster, the legend endured, leaving an indelible mark on anyone who gazed out upon Bear Lake's deep and mysterious depths.

In the summer of 1868 Joseph C. Rich penned a chilling account of the monster, sending his story to the Deseret News Newspaper. He recounted the Native American tradition of a water devil, a serpent-like creature that had terrorized the braves of old.

The story took a shocking turn when a number of white settlers came forward, declaring they had seen the creature with their own eyes. The Bear Lake Monster was no longer confined to the tales of the native people; it had become a living legend, a source of both fascination and fear.

One of the locals, S. M. Johnson had an encounter with the monster near South Eden, left him shaken. He mistook the creature's head and neck for the body of a man, but soon realized the truth – it was actually a strange animal with peculiar ear-like bunches on each side of its head.

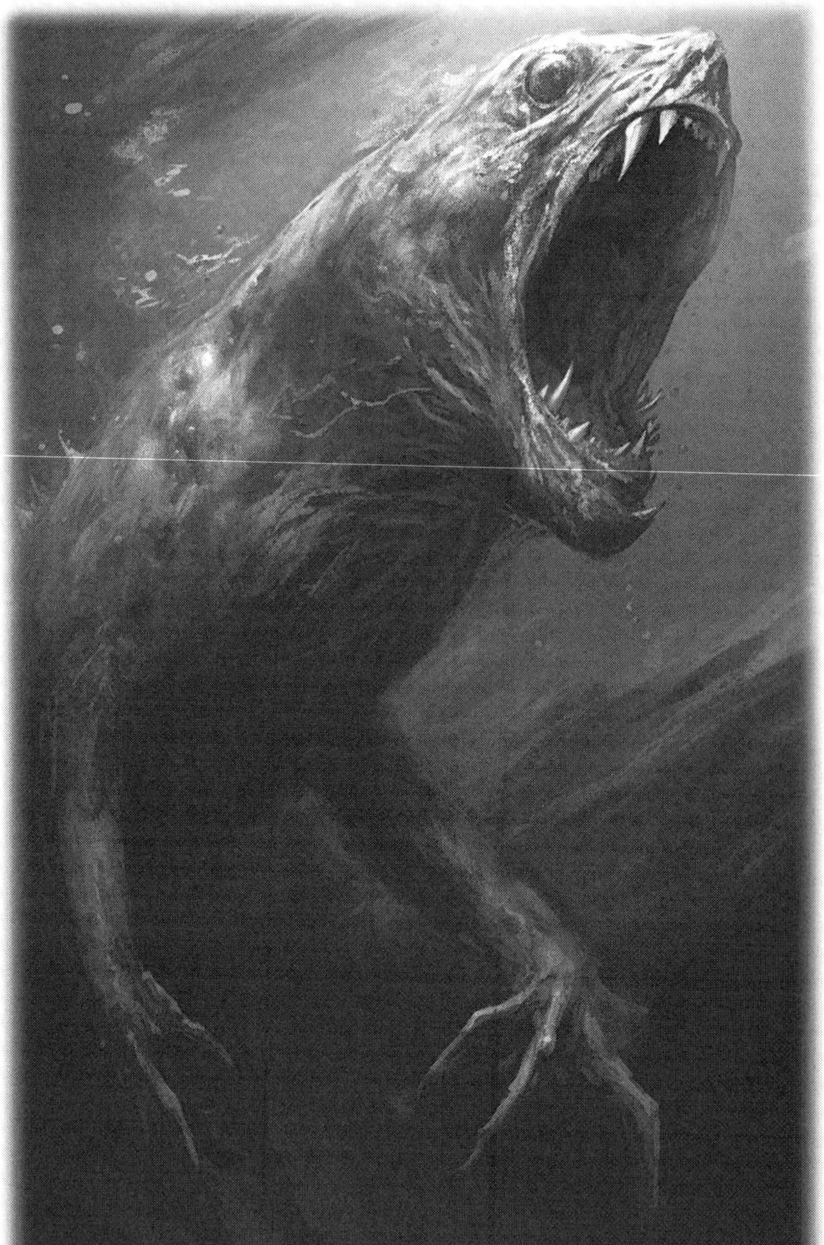

The sightings continued, witnessed by both men and women, who described a creature that moved with incredible speed, outpacing even a galloping horse. These were not mere stories; they were accounts given by reliable and prominent individuals.

The Bear Lake Monster's fame grew, and even the Dessert News ran a story from a correspondent on August 24, 1881, sparking great excitement. "While on the way from Fish Haven, a number of the party saw what they supposed was the celebrated Bear Lake monster. It was described as a large undulating body, with about 30 feet of exposed surface, of a light cream color, moving swiftly through the at a distance of three miles from the point of observation."

Skeptics questioned the veracity of the stories. Yet, the Indian legends persisted, speaking of creatures transformed by the Great Spirit, and the mystery deepened.

Since then, there have been other sightings. Descriptions of the monster varied, but common threads emerged – a brown or cream-colored body, a head reminiscent of an alligator or a walrus, large eyes, and strange ear-like bunches the size of pint cups. The monster's legs, about eighteen inches long, seemed to serve little purpose on land but facilitated its remarkable speed in the water.

The back part of the creature remained a mystery, forever concealed beneath the lake's surface. Was it all make-believe, or did the Bear Lake Monster truly dwell in the lake's depths? The answer remained elusive.

Oddly, Joseph Rich later recanted the stories, adding an aura of mystery to the legend. In recent years, the Bear Lake Monster has transformed into a tourist attraction, with the last reported sighting dating back to 2007.

As the legend of the Bear Lake Monster continues to capture the imagination, the truth remains hidden in the murky waters.

Sharlie of Payette Lake

Amidst the stunning landscapes of Idaho, Payette Lake is home to one of the region's most enduring enigmas — the legend of Sharlie, a cryptic creature that has stirred the imaginations of locals and visitors for generations.

Sharlie's story traces its origins to the late 19th century when settlers began to populate the lake's tranquil shores. This mysterious creature, often described as an aquatic serpent, is believed to dwell in the deep waters of the lake.

Tales of Sharlie have been passed down through the ages, with each generation adding its own unique spin to the legend.

Though the accounts of Sharlie vary, some recurring characteristics emerge from the stories. Witnesses describe it as a massive, eel-like entity, measuring anywhere from 20 to 40 feet in length. Its dark, scaly skin is said to gleam under the sunlight as it glides gracefully through the water. Sharlie is often depicted with a serpentine head, adorned with sharp teeth, and some accounts even liken it to the mythical Loch Ness Monster with a humpbacked appearance.

One of the most famous encounters with Sharlie dates back to 1920 when a group of people on a picnic reported spotting the creature during a lakeside outing. According to their story, they observed a colossal, shadowy form moving just beneath the water's surface. Startled by their presence, Sharlie swiftly vanished into the lake's depths, leaving only ripples on the surface.

Throughout the years, numerous other sightings have been reported. Witnesses claim to have glimpsed Sharlie from boats, kayaks, or along the lake's edge, recounting moments of both astonishment and trepidation. Some have even attested to hearing eerie, unexplained sounds originating from the water, further deepening the aura of mystique surrounding the legend.

While some speculate that Sharlie might be an unusually large trout or possibly a huge sturgeon, the legend remains firmly embedded in the region's culture. The town of McCall, situated on Payette Lake's shores, wholeheartedly embraces the legend, featuring a Sharlie parade in their winter festival.

Regardless of whether Sharlie truly dwells in the lake, the legend continues to flourish along Payette Lake.

The Lake Pend Oreille Paddler

In the heart of Idaho's unspoiled wilderness lies the enchanting Lake Pend Oreille, a vast expanse of crystalline waters framed by luxuriant forests and towering mountains. Its unparalleled beauty is rivalled only by the mysteries concealed beneath its surface, foremost among them being the fabled "Lake Pend Oreille Paddler."

For generations, the Paddler has been the subject of rumors among both locals and explorers. Accounts of this aquatic entity paint a picture reminiscent of ancient sea serpent myths—a sinuous, serpentine being whose movements ripple the lake's surface.

The legend of the Lake Pend Oreille Paddler traces its origins to a time when Idaho's wilderness remained largely uncharted, and encounters with this elusive creature were rare yet unforgettable. One of the earliest documented sightings occurred in the late 19th century when a group of fishermen bore witness to a colossal, shadowy form gliding silently beneath their boats. Its sheer size generated waves that echoed across the lake's surface.

Over the years, sporadic sightings and encounters with the Paddler have continued, often involving unwitting boaters, kayakers, or anglers who ventured further from the shore than they'd anticipated. Some recall glimpsing the creature's head and neck briefly emerging from the water, while others have recounted eerie, deep rumblings resonating from the lake's depths.

Local legends and indigenous folklore have spawned various theories about the Paddler's nature. Some regard it as a guardian spirit, intricately linked to the lake's ancient history. Others ponder whether it might be a relic of prehistoric times, a living fossil defying conventional scientific understanding.

Despite numerous expeditions and endeavors aimed at debunking its existence, the Lake Pend Oreille Paddler remains elusive. It retreats into the depths whenever spotted, leaving those fortunate enough to have glimpsed it with an enduring sense of wonder and curiosity.

Whether the Paddler is a creation of the imagination, a creature misidentified, or a genuine cryptid inhabiting the lake, it weaves an irresistible thread of mystery into the fabric of Idaho.

The Legend of Caddy the Sea Monster

The legend of Caddy, the sea monster of Washington State, is a tale as old as time, whispered among coastal communities for generations. Burrowed in the emerald waters of the Pacific Northwest, where dense forests meet the rugged shoreline, lies the enigmatic realm of Caddy.

According to local lore, Caddy is a colossal creature, a mysterious denizen of the deep, with a sinuous body that slithers through the dark abyss of the Salish Sea. Descriptions of this aquatic monster vary, but most agree on its snake-like form, often likened to a massive eel or a serpent of legendary proportions. Some witnesses claim to have glimpsed shimmering scales, while others speak of a leathery hide that glistens in the moonlight.

One of the earliest recorded sightings of Caddy dates back to 1933 when a group of fishermen off the coast of Victoria, British Columbia, reported a bizarre encounter. They described an enormous creature, roughly 60 feet long, as it rose from the depths, its head crowned with a frill of menacing spines. With eyes as dark as the abyss,

Caddy stared at them with an eerie, almost sentient intelligence, before gracefully slipping beneath the waves.

Over the years, the legend of Caddy grew, capturing the imaginations of locals and tourists alike. Tales of Caddy's antics soon became a staple of coastal storytelling. Some believe that Caddy is a guardian of the Salish Sea, a sentinel watching over its murky depths. Others see it as an omen, a harbinger of storms and turbulent waters.

Intriguingly, numerous sightings and photographs of strange, serpentine creatures have been reported throughout the region, fueling the belief that Caddy may not be alone in its aquatic domain. These accounts have sparked debate among scientists and cryptozoologists, who continue to explore the mysteries of the Salish Sea.

While skeptics argue that these sightings can be attributed to misidentifications of known marine animals or simply tall tales spun around a campfire, the legend of Caddy endures, woven into the cultural fabric of Washington State. It has inspired countless works of art, literature, and even a few daring expeditions to uncover the truth behind the strange sea monster.

Beware the Qalupalik

In the remote reaches of Alaska, where icy waters and towering glaciers dominate the landscape, a chilling legend has been passed down through generations. It is the legend of the Qalupalik, a mysterious and fearsome creature that haunts the waters of the Arctic Ocean.

The Qalupalik is said to be a monstrous sea creature, part human and part sea creature, with long, seaweed-like hair and greenish, scaly skin. Its eyes are said to glow an eerie blue, and its long, bony fingers end in sharp, claw-like nails. This creature is said to live beneath the ice-covered waters of the Arctic, lurking just beneath the surface, waiting for unsuspecting prey such as small children.

According to Inuit legend, the Qalupalik preys upon disobedient kids who venture too close to the water's edge. They say that it lures them in with a mesmerizing, hypnotic song, beckoning them to come closer. Once a child is within reach, the Qalupalik snatches them with its long, cold fingers and drags them beneath the surface, never to be seen again.

The story of the Qalupalik serves as a cautionary tale for Inuit children, warning them to obey their parents and stay away from the dangerous waters of the Arctic. It is a story that has been told around campfires for centuries, instilling a healthy dose of fear and respect for the power of the ocean.

But some say that the Qalupalik is more than just a story, that it is a real and ancient creature that still haunts the waters of Alaska to this day. There have been reports of strange sightings and eerie sounds emanating from the depths of the Arctic Ocean, leading some to believe that the Qalupalik is not just a legend but a living, breathing monster.

Whether the Qalupalik is a creature of myth or reality, one thing is certain: it continues to cast a chilling shadow over the icy waters of Alaska.

The Keelut

In the desolate, bone-chilling expanse of the Arctic wilderness, a name strikes terror into the hearts of all who hear it – the Keelut. This malevolent entity is no ordinary legend; it is the embodiment of pure evil.

The Keelut is an abomination, a hulking beast that takes the form of a colossal, ebony nightmare. With its grotesque, hairless body, it exudes an aura of relentless cruelty. The darkness of its furless skin seems to absorb even the feeblest light, leaving it to haunt the frozen night like a wraith.

What makes this creature all the more sinister is its eerie ability to vanish into the snow, leaving no trace of its presence. Its tracks, obscured by its dark magic, vanish beneath the frozen blanket, granting it the perfect advantage in stalking its unsuspecting victims. It watches and waits, a silent specter of death.

But do not be deceived by the notion of this being as merely a physical predator. The Keelut is not bound by the laws of nature; it is a spirit of the Netherworld, an unholy force that hungers for human souls. It materializes with a blood-curdling purpose – to hunt and to devour.

The stories that have been passed down through generations describe its malice in the darkest of terms. Encountering the Keelut is not just a brush with danger; it is a descent into madness. To glimpse those malevolent eyes is to invite doom. The Keelut, with its unnerving presence, leaves victims disoriented, helpless, and paralyzed by sheer terror.

Hoaxes

Georgie

The legend of the Lake George Monster, affectionately known as "Georgie," unfolded in the heart of the Adirondack region of western New York, on the waters of Lake George in 1904.

The genesis of Georgie can be traced back to a friendly competition between two men, artist Harry Watrous and newspaper editor Colonel William Mann. The challenge they set for themselves was simple: who could reel in the most impressive trout from Lake George? Little did they know that this rivalry would lead to the creation of one of the most entertaining and enduring legends in the annals of American hoaxes.

In an amusing twist of fate, Mann managed to outwit Watrous in their fishing contest. As Mann's boat sailed by, he triumphantly held up what appeared to be an enormous 30-to-40-pound trout, seemingly securing his victory. Watrous, humbled and somewhat embarrassed, accepted his defeat. However, the artist later uncovered Mann's had deceived him. The colossal fish was nothing more than a cleverly crafted hand-carved wooden fish.

Undeterred by his rival's prank, Watrous hatched a plan of his own. He aimed to outdo Mann's fake fish with a spectacle that would amaze and bewilder. Thus, Georgie was born from a ten-foot cedar log. Watrous transformed one end of the log into an eerie spectacle. Its jaws opened wide, revealing large eyes, gnarled red fangs, and a set of whiskers made from frayed hemp rope. The monster's countenance bore a surreal semblance to the mythical sea creatures of lore.

To complete his illusion, Watrous devised an ingenious mechanism. A 100-foot-long rope was threaded through a pulley affixed to the log's end, and it was anchored to a stone, submerged beneath the water. This setup allowed Watrous to manipulate Georgie's appearances, raising and lowering the creature at will. The monster was poised to make its dramatic debut on the shores of Lake George.

The day arrived, and Mann went to the lake with some friends. Unbeknownst to them, Watrous lay in wait, ready to unleash his aquatic marvel. As Mann's boat approached the spot, Watrous pulled the rope, causing Georgie to rise ominously from the depths.

The monstrous apparition emerged with a dramatic flourish, its head quaking as if shaking off the aquatic slumber. Mann's guests were met with a vision both astounding and disconcerting. One guest's scream rang through the air, while another frantically brandished her parasol and began striking the man-made monster. Mann himself exclaimed, "Good God, what is it?" repeatedly, his voice trembling as he gazed upon the fantastical creation.

The hoax proved to be an instant success, and the legend of Georgie, the Lake George Monster, was born. Watrous continued to refine and enhance the ruse, moving the monster to various points around the lake to maintain the illusion. News of the sea serpent's existence spread like wildfire, capturing the imagination of locals and visitors alike.

However, Watrous couldn't resist revealing the truth of his monstrous creation. Thirty years later, he unveiled the secret behind Georgie, much to the amusement of those who had been captivated by the legendary creature.

Watrous's cunning craftsmanship and ingenuity brought Georgie to life, and as the years passed, the Lake George Monster found its final resting place as an exhibit at the Clifton F. West Historical Museum in Hague, New York. Forever preserved, Georgie's legacy lives on, a testament to the playful spirit of human creativity and the enduring power of a well-executed prank.

Is She Human or Fish?

In 1838 and 1839, a remarkable event known as the Great London Trainway Exhibition captured the imagination of people all across the United States with its extraordinary assortment of curiosities. This traveling carnival sideshow was ingeniously housed inside train cars that were parked on sidetracks, and it traveled from one town to the next, mesmerizing audiences from California to South Carolina. What made this exhibition particularly captivating was the clever ruse employed by its promoter.

As the spectacle arrived in each new location, the promoter utilized advertisements in local newspapers, creating a buzz that piqued the curiosity of the townsfolk. These advertisements featured enticing buzzwords such as "Sharks," "Headless Girl," and "Mermaid." Some of the ads were straightforward, featuring an image that appeared to be a mermaid, accompanied by text designed to intrigue, such as "Do Mermaids live?" or "Is she human or fish?" These advertisements successfully generated a sense of wonder and anticipation among the locals who were eager to witness these wonders for themselves, all for a modest admission fee of just ten cents.

> **SELMA, ALABAMA**
> FRIDAY—SATURDAY
> SUNDAY
> November 24, 25, 26
> IN RAILROAD CAR AT
> SOUTHERN DEPOT
> Other Strange Sights Include:
>
> SHARKS!
> HEADLESS
> GIRL!
> MERMAID
> —ALIVE!
> 68-TON
> WHALE!
>
> *The* GREATEST EDUCATIONAL EXHIBITION OF ALL TIME!
>
> DID YOU EVER SEE A WHALE?
> Open 2 P.M. to 10 P.M., Daily
> Admission: 10c to Everyone

The centerpiece of this traveling train car show was an astonishing spectacle: a massive "Sea Monster." Despite its fantastical appearance, this majestic creature was, in reality, an embalmed carcass of a 68-ton, 55-foot-long whale that had been skillfully captured by Captain Jack Lampe of the renowned Eureka Whaling Company off the coast of California.

Among the other exhibits was Madam Sirwell's Flea Circus, a genuine marvel in its own right. In this extraordinary display, a troupe of fifty trained fleas showcased their incredible talents: kicking miniature footballs, juggling, pulling tiny carts, and even competing in races. To create an air of authenticity, these insects were affixed to props or delicately suspended by minuscule wires. Clever techniques, such as subtle heat application, were employed to craft the illusion flawlessly, effectively conveying the impression that the fleas were indeed moving and performing daring stunts.

However, the two most popular attractions in the sideshow were The Great Serpentina, the Human Mermaid, and Nina Sontata, the Headless Girl. These two human oddities drew crowds to the exhibition in droves.

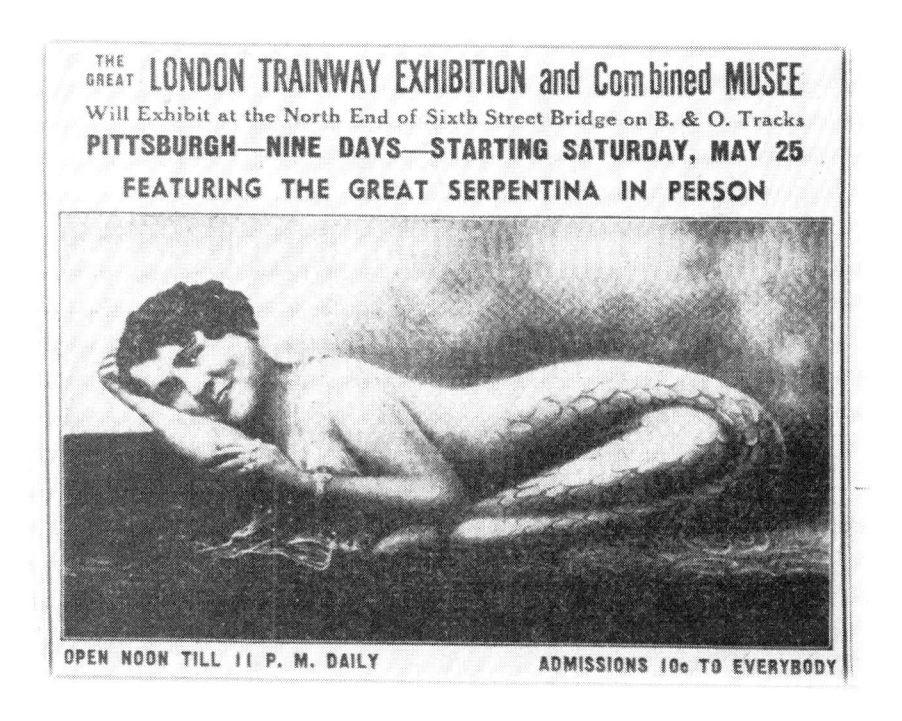

THE GREAT LONDON TRAINWAY EXHIBITION and Combined MUSEE
Will Exhibit at the North End of Sixth Street Bridge on B. & O. Tracks
PITTSBURGH—NINE DAYS—STARTING SATURDAY, MAY 25
FEATURING THE GREAT SERPENTINA IN PERSON

OPEN NOON TILL 11 P. M. DAILY   ADMISSIONS 10c TO EVERYBODY

In late April 1839, when the sideshow arrived in St. Louis, the entire town was abuzz with anticipation. The exhibition had piqued the curiosity of a police detective's wife, who convinced her husband to accompany her and witness the strange woman without a head.

As the policeman explored the various train cars, he began to suspect that something was awry and alerted a sergeant. On April 28, nine detectives descended upon the sidetrack near Vandeventer and Tower Grove Avenue, where the Headless Girl and Human Mermaid were being showcased. In the raid, the police discovered that the Headless Woman actually had a head and an identity. She was revealed to be Myrtle Jones, a 22-year-old woman from Ruskin, Texas.

The Human Mermaid turned out to be Mary Krasinski, an ordinary divorced housewife from Ohio, who wore an elaborate costume. In exchange for dedicating a few days of her week to this role, Mary received a modest $20 per week (equivalent to $450 in 2024).

The police acted swiftly, arresting Myrtle, Mary, the promoter, and another associate, all of whom were charged with obtaining money under false pretenses. While in jail, Myrtle provided insights into the intricate workings behind the Headless Woman illusion. The spectacle unfolded inside of a small booth, where Myrtle lay on her back. Using hidden mirrors, the glow emitted by a powerful 500-watt electrical lamp inside a hidden compartment created the illusion of her headless form.

In the aftermath, each member of the sideshow was ordered to pay a small fine. Following their appearance before the judge, the troupe promptly dismantled their show and quickly headed to the next town. In light of her arrest, the Human Mermaid distanced herself from the name Nina Sontata, adopting the moniker Arcadia, the Human Mermaid, from that point onward. Despite the hiccup in St. Louis, the Great London Trainway Exhibition continued their traveling show for a few more years before the promoter finally went bankrupt.

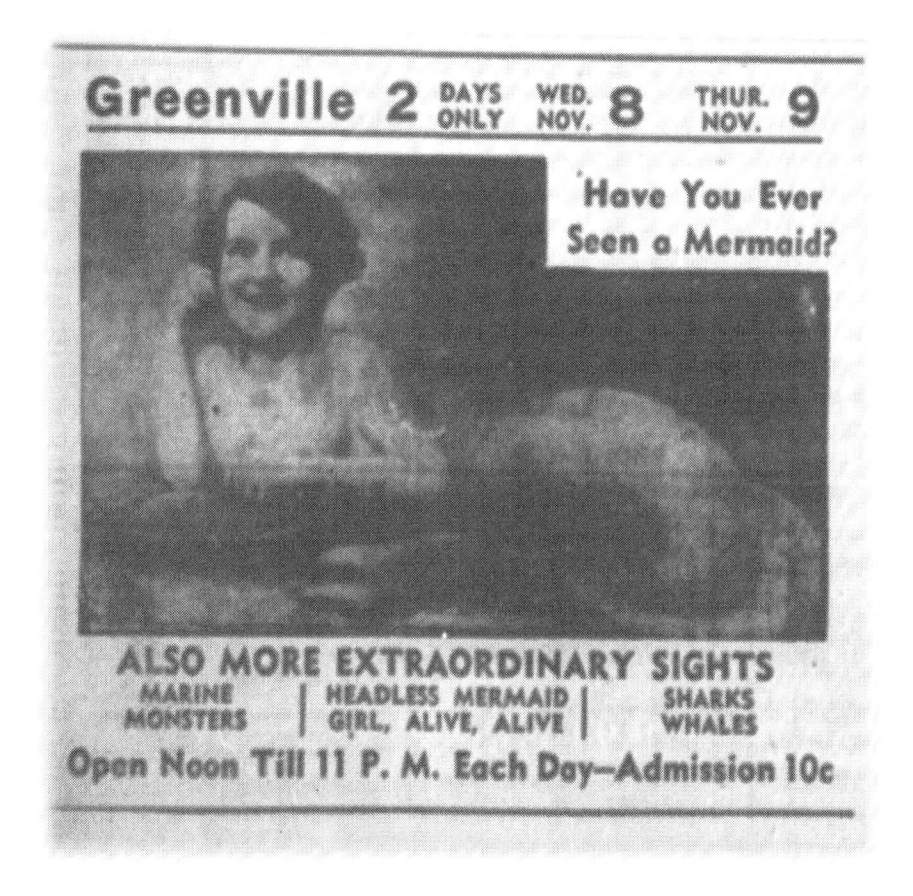

Greenville 2 DAYS ONLY WED. NOV. 8 THUR. NOV. 9

Have You Ever Seen a Mermaid?

ALSO MORE EXTRAORDINARY SIGHTS
MARINE MONSTERS | HEADLESS MERMAID GIRL, ALIVE, ALIVE | SHARKS WHALES

Open Noon Till 11 P. M. Each Day—Admission 10c

The Loveland Frogman

The legend of the Loveland Frog, a cryptid known for its frog-like appearance and peculiar encounters in Loveland, Ohio. It's a tale that has intrigued and mystified residents of the area for decades, with some peculiar twists along the way.

The Loveland Frog made its first appearance in the early-1970s, marking the genesis of this unusual legend. This frog-like cryptid, standing at approximately 4 feet tall and known for walking on two legs, became the focus of local folklore. However, the story took an intriguing twist in 1972 when a Loveland police officer reported a startling encounter with the creature.

Officer Ray Shockey was driving on Riverside Drive near a factory and the Little Miami River one night. It was around 1:00 a.m. when an unidentified creature scurried across the road in front of his vehicle. Illuminated by the headlights, the creature was fully visible, and it defied easy explanation. Shockey described it as being 3 to 4 feet in length and weighing approximately 50 to 75 pounds. Its leathery skin and peculiar behavior added to the eerie encounter. The creature appeared to crouch like a frog before momentarily standing upright and making its way over a guardrail, vanishing towards the river.

Two weeks later, the Loveland Frogman legend picked up steam when another police officer, Mark Matthews, reported a sighting in the same area as Shockey's encounter. Matthews observed an unidentified creature crouched along the road, but his response was significantly different from his colleague's. In an instant, he quickly pulled out his gun and shot the creature. He then picked up the remains of the Loveland Frog and placed its lifeless body in the trunk of his car, intending to present it as evidence to Officer Shockey.

Upon closer examination of the creature, Matthews realized that it was not the mysterious frogman that the legend had led them to believe. Instead, it was a large iguana without a tail, measuring almost four feet in length. Matthews speculated that the iguana had likely been someone's pet that had either escaped or was released when it grew too large for its owner to handle.

This revelation brought a dose of reality to the fantastical tale of the Loveland Frog. What had once been a mysterious cryptid was, in this instance, a misunderstood creature that shared little resemblance to the mythical frogman of local legend.

Made in the USA
Columbia, SC
12 May 2025